Just Another Day

Just Another Day

Patricia Fawcett

ROBERT HALE · LONDON

ISBN 978-0-7090-9322-0

Robert Hale Limited
Clerkenwell House
Clerkenwell Green
London EC1R 0HT

www.halebooks.com

2 4 6 8 10 9 7 5 3 1

To Tracy and Barnstable ladies.

With my thanks for the coffee, cake and conversation.

Typeset in 11/16pt New Century Schoolbook
Printed and bound in Great Britain by
the MPG Books Group

Chapter One

'I FEEL TERRIBLE imposing myself on you like this,' Francesca said, sitting beside Selina in the people-carrier. Despite its size, akin to an army tank, there was still hardly any room to sit in it because of the children's seats, buggies and all the assorted paraphernalia that children bring with them. 'You have enough to do. Are you sure Clive doesn't mind?' A thought struck her suddenly. 'You have asked him, haven't you?'

'Of course. I do believe I mentioned it although he never listens. He's in a world of his own most of the time.'

'Oh, Selina.'

'Not to worry. He's never at home anyway,' she went on. 'You know Clive, he practically lives at that office of his. Sometimes he doesn't get home until ten o'clock and he hardly ever sees the boys. When was the last time he read them a bedtime story? Who is this strange man they ask me.'

'No they don't. You're exaggerating. He's very good with them.'

'You're right and come to think of it I'm pushed myself to find time for the bedtime story. However, with all the hours he puts in if I didn't know him better I'd say he was having an affair with his secretary but thank God she's not the type. She's fifty if she's a day and she has a problem with her feet, poor darling, so she has to wear those dreadful shoes.'

Francesca smiled, grateful to Selina for trying to lighten things up, and aware too that she was as desperately uncomfortable as Francesca herself was with this awful situation. As to Clive having an affair, the idea was preposterous; Selina's marriage to the gentle giant was as solid as they come. Quite obviously though she had neglected to mention to her husband that she had invited Francesca to stay for a while and that made Francesca feel awkward.

She bit her lip and sighed, coming perilously close to asking Selina to pull over right away and let her out.

Selina, astute as always, read her mind.

'Will you stop worrying? You are such a worrier.'

'Is it surprising judging by what's happened to me recently?'

'I'm saying this for the very last time so listen to me. It's no problem at all having you to stay for a while so do shut up about it. We are looking forward to it,' Selina said, taking her hand off the wheel and patting Francesca's knee. 'You know how much Cosmo adores you. It's the least I can do, darling. I can't bear to think of you all alone in that house and I don't want David coming back to haunt me because I'm not looking after you.'

'He wouldn't dare. You do know he was scared stiff of you. He said that Clive deserved a medal for taking you on. Only joking of course,' she said quickly, sensing that her comment had not gone down well. 'You know he thought the world of you.'

'No, he thought the world of *you*, Francesca.'

She admired Selina greatly; she was one of those working mother miracles who take multi-tasking to a new height. They were about the same age, early forties, but that's where the similarity ended. Selina was a tall coolly attractive blue-eyed blonde, a solicitor specializing in family law, appropriate because she was mummy herself to three boys under five, Crispin, Cosmo and baby Charles.

As if that wasn't enough she was also keeper of a menagerie of small pets and wife to a successful husband who adored her and yet here she was finding the time and space to try to nurse a numb Francesca back to some sort of sanity. Selina had turned up trumps when all her other so-called friends had simply faded away, although to be fair to them it was probably just because they were embarrassed and didn't know how to handle it.

With no other plans and hating the thought of staying in David's house on her own – almost afraid to go into the sitting-room and look at the very chair where he breathed his last – Francesca reluctantly took up Selina's offer to stay with them on a short-term basis until she got herself together again.

'The traffic today is bloody horrendous,' Selina said, squeezing the car through a gap to take her rightful place at the lights, stopping and glaring at a helmeted man on a bike. 'I hate cyclists. I keep telling Clive that it is far too dangerous for him to cycle to work and to breathe in all the traffic fumes; they must surely counteract the good it does him. You must speak to him about it, Francesca. He might take notice of you.'

'No thank you. I'm not getting involved.'

'I didn't think you would. You hate confrontation, don't you?'

'That doesn't sound like a compliment?'

'It wasn't meant to. The trouble with you is you're much too nice and smiley and you don't get anywhere in this world by being too nice or too smiley,' Selina said, setting off with scant consideration for the poor cyclist at her side. 'You just get trampled on, that's all. You have to develop an edge to your personality to succeed.'

'Oh I don't know.' Francesca felt bound to argue the point. 'I didn't do too badly in my job. I made it to a Senior Creative Director post, Selina, and I was never knowingly nasty to anybody.'

'You wouldn't know how.' Selina grunted, acknowledging that she had lost that point and changing the subject abruptly. 'Have you thought anymore about what you are going to do?'

'About what?' Francesca frowned. These days she was in such a daze that even simple questions eluded her.

'Well, for one, are you going back to work? Are you going to reclaim your job as *Senior Creative Director*?'

Francesca glanced sharply at her, at the way she emphasized the title, but Selina blithely carried on. 'I don't mean this very minute obviously, but when you've come round a bit. You were so good at the job that they must be missing you like hell. What have they said?' Selina asked, approaching the question most people were afraid to ask in her usual bulldozer fashion. 'I know you resigned and they gave you a farewell do and everything but your circumstances have changed now that you're no longer going to move up north so they should recognize that. Do you think you could have your old job back? If that's what you want to do of course.'

'They've already said I can have it back.' Francesca sighed, stopping herself from stamping on an imaginary brake as Selina approached a junction a little too fast for her liking. 'But I've said no. I can't go back there. They'll all be far too sympathetic and I can't face it.'

'Take it from me, they'll be sympathetic for one day and then it will be business as usual.'

Francesca turned abruptly away to gaze out of the car window at a world she was no longer seeing properly. Selina was probably right, but she wasn't going to let her dictate what she should or should not do. In any case, it would be too difficult to go back because they had wasted no time in appointing her deputy to her old job and it would cause no end of complications if she returned. Nor did she want to deprive poor Lorna of the opportunity that she had been waiting so long to grasp.

'I hope you've told Clive he needn't treat me like bone china in case I fall apart. I'm absolutely fine if people just pretend it hasn't happened.'

'You needn't worry. Believe me, darling, he'll hardly notice you're there. If he's not at the office, he's sitting in his study doing something fearfully exciting with figures. He's a walking calculator. His brain must be computer tuned.' She shot a glance at her. 'Have you told the office you're not going back?'

'Yes I've told them. Reading between the lines, I think it was a relief all round. I have to move on, but I need time to think so I'm not rushing into another job and a break from advertising would also be good, anyway. It's so frantic and stressful.'

'I always thought that it wasn't really the job for you,' Selina said. 'You're not the type. They're all either hard-faced bitches or guys with huge egos and you just didn't seem to fit in. You're too nice.'

'Will you stop saying that? It's not true anyway. I worked with some lovely people.'

'The trouble with you is that you have to see the good in everyone. How lucky though that you don't actually need to work,' Selina said lightly but, in her sensitive condition Francesca detected a slight irritation in her tone. Suddenly coming into money was not without its difficulties. She knew what people were saying. It did not look good David dying so early into the marriage and at his funeral they, his acquaintances and colleagues, looked at her as if it was somehow her fault, as if she, twenty years his junior, had exhausted him with her sexual demands. That was so far from the truth it was laughable for it was David who had come close to exhausting her.

It was just one of those things. A sudden massive heart attack and nobody was to blame, but try telling that to his friends. They blamed her, she knew that, but she had hoped that Selina wasn't one of them. She could not help it if David had left her comfortably off and it was not her fault either if Selina and Clive chose to live in this neighbourhood where the average price of a house was close to a million pounds. A pair of high flyers, they earned a lot between them, but they spent a lot too. Selina was always grumbling about money or rather the lack of it although that did not stop her from shopping like a woman possessed. Today she was wearing fabulous designer high-heeled shoes hardly suitable for driving the tank but she managed it with aplomb much as she managed everything.

Things, she prophesied, would only get worse once they had to start forking out big time for full-time private education. The charge for the little nursery Crispin and Cosmo attended was sky-high already, although it was perfect and Selina had not been averse to a little underhand dealing to secure them a place. It was a cut-throat world she explained to Francesca who had been more than a little horrified at the tactics and it was every mummy for herself.

With Selina's financial fussing uppermost in her mind Francesca knew she had to make an offer at least to pay her way whilst she was staying with them.

'Look, Selina, let's get one thing straight. I don't expect you to put me up for free,' she said, embarrassed to be saying it, but feeling it was necessary. 'Please let me contribute something whilst I'm staying with you. Let me get the weekly shop or buy you a case of wine.'

'The case of wine is tempting but for God's sake, Francesca, don't be daft.' Selina turned her attention briefly from the road ahead to smile at her. 'And don't you dare say that in front of Clive. We wouldn't dream of it. You are a friend and you are most welcome to stay for as long as you feel you need to. You only eat like a sparrow anyway. Look at you, there's nothing to you.'

'I've lost weight but that's because of all this,' Francesca said defensively because Selina was making it sound as if she was anorexic. 'The last thing you feel like is eating, believe me.'

'Of course it is. I shall make lots of filling pasta dishes and you'll soon pile on the pounds. As I said to Clive, if this had to happen to anybody then the best person it could happen to is Francesca. You've coped beautifully, darling. You were so gracious and composed and smiling at the funeral whilst I was a complete wreck.'

'I still can't believe it.' Francesca stared out unseeingly as Selina signalled and turned the final corner. 'It's all happened so quickly. One minute we were planning the move up to Yorkshire, the next ...'

'I know. He chose a very inconvenient moment to die. Typical of him.'

'I'm sure he didn't plan it.'

'Of course not although I am sure he would not have wanted to have a long drawn out illness so you can take comfort from that. I'm sure we would all go for the quick option given half a chance.'

'Selina, please ...'

'Sorry but it's true. Anyway, look on the bright side, it's saved you moving up to Yorkshire. Be honest Francesca, your heart wasn't in that move, was it?'

'I would have got used to it,' she said, anxious to defend herself even though Selina had hit a nerve. 'You should have seen the house we were going to buy. You would have loved it.'

'I would have only loved it if I could have moved it to London, darling. Catch me living up there.'

'It was a mansion. Two and a half acres. Goodness knows how we would have managed the upkeep. I said it was far too big, but you know what David was like.'

'I do indeed. You forget I knew him for much longer than you. Here we are. Home sweet home.' Selina swung the car into the drive. 'We've time for a coffee and a slice of chocolate cake before the boys get back. God knows we need something to cheer ourselves up.' She made no attempt to get out of the car, curtains of fair hair falling across her face as she hung her head, voice cracking a little. 'You mustn't mind me, Francesca. I know I joke and everything but it's just a front I put on. I still can't believe that he's dead either. He was so vibrant, so full of life.'

She glanced at Francesca, her eyes suddenly filling with tears, causing Francesca to step out quickly and head towards the house before it became a full-on Selina blub.

'Sorry, it just came over me,' Selina said, sniffing as she caught her up, fumbling with house keys. 'You're being so brave, darling, and I have no idea how you keep smiling.'

'It's what he would have wanted. Stiff upper lip and all that. In any case, my smiling helps other people.'

Selina looked unconvinced. 'He really has a colossal nerve doing this to you leaving you all on your own like this. He could at least have waited until you'd got yourself up to the new house and settled in. I can say this to you because we both loved him but you know as well as I do that, underneath that charming exterior, that husband of yours was one selfish pig. And if he's up there,' she gazed heavenwards. 'I want him to jolly well know it.'

There was a moment's shocked silence when even Selina realized she might have gone one step too far.

Rarely surprised by her friend, but knowing she meant well, Francesca laughed it off and, after a moment with her composure regained, so did Selina.

Chapter Two

IT WAS AN unlikely match, destined to be short and sweet.

People were reluctant to say it out loud, but Francesca knew that this was what they had been thinking and, although many of his friends and colleagues were far too polite and respected David too much to voice it, she suspected there must have been considerable raising of eyebrows and shaking of heads when their engagement was announced. Francesca was overjoyed, showing off the precious antique ring to the girls at work, smiling at the expected shrieks of delight, happy to ignore what they might be saying behind her back.

As a man in his early sixties, if David had followed the usual pattern his wife would be close to that age, maybe a well pre-served blonde from a privileged background who would wear expensive dresses or casual gear with equal aplomb. Content to be a homemaker rather than a career woman, she would be mother to a batch of grown-up sons and daughters, all of whom would have done incredibly well in their careers. She would undoubtedly be a grandmother by now and she would be at her happiest surrounded by dogs and grandchildren, in that order, and she would complement David beautifully. She would be able to up her game when required, talk with ease to the other high-ranking members of his profession – David Porter was a senior barrister – and all his friends would agree that Felicity or Pippa was a good sort with an excellent pedigree and wasn't David lucky to have her.

Francesca, petite and softly spoken with light brown hair and eyes the colour of dark chocolate was young enough to be his daughter. Worse, she was a senior executive in the world of advertising, could boast of no grand family connections and, therefore, did not fit the bill socially at all. That was why she turned down his proposal at first, laughing to cover up her surprise.

David did not return her laughter for he was deadly serious.

'I'm not doing this lightly, my sweet,' he told her, taking her hand in his. They were in the candlelit depths of the restaurant, a table for two in a discreet lovers' corner and she might have guessed it was coming. She might have guessed from the suppressed excitement in his eyes from the moment he had picked her up that evening. She had fussed over what to wear, maybe suspecting it would be no ordinary dinner, and she had chosen a dark grey softly draped dress and, because it was cold outside, a pretty faux-fur wrap.

It was David's favourite restaurant where he had dined alone for many years and she sensed that the waiting staff was collectively holding its breath, poised to bring the champagne as soon as David gave the signal. 'I've thought about this long and hard and more than anything I want you to be my wife, Francesca. I've never done this before and you have to say yes or you'll break my heart, my darling.'

'But we've only known each other a little while,' she protested stopping short of withdrawing her hand and calling it ridiculous. She looked down at his hand on hers. He had nice hands and was not afraid to have them professionally manicured, a starched white cuff peeped out from the sleeve of his suit, anchored with expensive gold cuff-links. David had such style. 'We've only known each other a few months,' she repeated anxiously. 'Where on earth has this come from? I didn't think you were the impulsive type, David.'

'You don't know me.'

That was true and it was another good reason why she must say no. Helplessly she looked round for support, but they were unobserved in their quiet corner and he was waiting for an answer, a confident look in his unusual greenish-grey eyes. David was not used to people saying no to him.

'I'm very flattered,' she began and at that she saw the first signs of doubt in those eyes. 'But I can't give you an answer here and now. I need to think about it. I don't like to say it, but have you considered the age thing? I'm a lot younger than you.'

'Don't you dare use that as an excuse,' he said, voice low. 'You know that doesn't matter in the least. It didn't matter last night, did it? I didn't disappoint you, did I?'

She smiled, squeezed his hand.

'Thank God for that. I don't feel my age, my sweet, if that helps. I feel about forty or so. Anyway, when you get down to the nitty gritty we love each other and that's all that matters. I don't give a fig what anybody else thinks. I'd give up the lot of them, all those outrageous friends of mine, for you.'

It was sweet of him but how, in all honesty, could she marry him? They had absolutely nothing in common and, sitting there in that restaurant that evening, she regretted letting it go this far by accepting his first invitation to dinner. That had been mistake number one and the second had been allowing herself to be swept along by the whirlwind nature of their romance. Never before had she been made to feel like a lady. David treated the ladies with a respect and old-fashioned courtesy that was mostly lacking in younger men and even though she knew she ought not to allow that to sway her she could not help it.

It felt wonderful.

What was she doing, stringing a man like David along? Her last serious relationship had lasted a couple of years when she was fresh out of college. She and Andrew had been serious about each other and the break-up, even if she had instigated it, had been hurtful. It had taken her ages to recover and, very much off men, her thirties had passed in a flash with just the occasional romantic episode as she concentrated on building her career.

She had resigned herself to being alone, although resigned wasn't the right word because she had been quite content living the single life even if everyone else thought she ought not to be, but then along came David and all she wanted was to be with him.

It was a mystery why they seemed to hit it off so well for she did not share his interests which was supposed to be one of the main areas for compatibility in a relationship. For one thing, she knew nothing about contemporary art, one of his passions, but she tried her best to feign interest going along with him to various exhibitions. He had become interested in the work of talented young artists and had started to build a collection and become something of a benefactor. Standing at his side, clutching a glass of champagne, trying her best to show some appreciation of the art on display she was appalled at how stupid she felt. She was not stupid, far from it, nor was she a shy teenager but rather a normally confident woman used to speaking to people – all kinds of people – as an essential part of her job.

How could she marry him?

He was so out of her league, a generation and a world apart.

She worried that, deprived of her own father at a young age, she was actively if subconsciously looking for a father figure and that was a tough one to admit to.

She was not part of his law scene and, once they were engaged and considered to be an item she envisaged dreadful dinner parties where nobody knew quite what to make of her, the wives of his contemporaries all being so much older, upper crust women who to their credit welcomed her with a smile into their exclusive little circle. Tellingly, however, they dropped her like a hot potato immediately after his death. They might privately feel David had taken leave of his senses, but they kept that to themselves, taking on a maternal role, all seemingly delighted that at last the man they thought would never ever marry was about to take the plunge.

'David, you old fox,' she heard one of them say in a flirty manner. 'I never thought you had it in you. And isn't she just a darling?'

Looking at the woman, seeing the faint smile, she wondered if she had been one of David's previous conquests.

How could she marry him?

Had she taken leave of *her* senses?

There was nobody she could talk to about it, no girlfriend with whom she could have a cosy chat. There was their mutual friend Selina of course, but Selina was like a devoted sister to him, had been responsible for introducing them and Francesca did not think she would get a balanced view from her. There was Izzy, too, her old school-friend back in Devon, but their long distance telephone conversations had faded away now that she was a busy mum and this wasn't the sort of thing she could discuss on the phone anyway.

On the plus side David would have got on well with her father Geoffrey. Her father had taught History at a small private school and had been the sort of quiet scholarly type of man, immersed in books and rarely surfacing to face the real world, who, shy and a little awkward himself, would have been drawn to David's charm and zeal.

But her father was not here and she hadn't a clue whether or not he was still alive and even though she had once thought of trying to trace him she had dismissed the idea for it might well open a can of worms. In any case, it wasn't worth the effort for what kind of man would abandon his only daughter as he had. It was the abandonment that hurt the most and even though she now knew she was not to blame in any way, she had worried as a little girl that his leaving was all her fault.

She carried a heavily laden guilt bag around with her. She had once tried visualization therapy, been sent into a kind of trance by a softly encouraging voice and been told to drop the bag off on an imaginary bench in the middle of a beautiful imaginary sun-kissed garden. It hadn't quite worked and somewhere along the line she had returned and picked up the blessed thing again.

So, in the end, whether or not she accepted David's proposal was entirely up to her and she made the decision to turn him down that evening in that restaurant and as a result the champagne never materialized and they left early abandoning dessert. David took it on the chin but she could not fail to notice the annoyed glances the waiting staff showed her as if she had somehow spoilt their evening too.

'I refuse to accept your answer. I'll think of this as a temporary set-back. I'm not going to let you go,' David warned her as they exited the restaurant. He placed a hand on the small of her back as they waited for the taxi. 'I've just taken you by surprise that's all and, of course, you need time to think about it. When you do think about it then you will change your mind. It's taken me forty years to find my lady love and I have no intention of letting you walk away from me.'

His lady love? She had laughed at that but the expression had a quiet old-fashioned ring to it that also delighted her. He was a charming man, but there were many reasons for turning him down and in the cold light of day he would see that she was right to do so. In fact, she made up her mind there and then that she would have to extricate herself from the relationship as gently as she could for she had no wish to hurt him.

But David would not take no for an answer.

He was true to his word, wearing her down eventually, using all the skills he used in court, discounting all the increasingly idiotic reasons she came up with until at last she said yes. He was quite right. It did not matter that he was so much older because the sheer verve of his personality mesmerized her. People sat up and took notice when David spoke, but then he was used to people hanging onto his every word. His presence in a room was powerful, his intellect alarming, his confidence verging on a sexy arrogance and yet, although he knew so much about everything, in some ways he knew nothing. He knew very little about women and as a lifelong bachelor was set in his ways.

What people could not understand, what she could barely understand herself was that she had fallen in love with him. It was as simple as that. He was a suitably distinguished looking man with a shaggy head of grey hair a touch longer than might be expected, the slightest swagger, a twinkle in his eyes and a rare, but devastating smile.

That was her David.

He was always immaculately clad with a wardrobe full of bespoke suits – his tailors in Mayfair sent a condolence card saying he had been one of their most valued clients and would be sorely missed – and she had never seen a man who looked as good as David when he was wearing black tie. He ate sen-

sibly, drank in moderation and, although he laughed at his contemporaries who had a gym membership he was careful to
watch his weight, his only vice was to enjoy an after-dinner
cigar. It puzzled Francesca that he had taken so long to find a
wife for he was handsome enough and must have been seen as
a real catch when he was younger. He had, he told her, been
too involved with his other love, his work, to have any time for
courting the fair sex – his words – and by the time he achieved
what he had set out to achieve in his career it came as a shock
to realize he was getting old and possibly past it.

No way was he past it. He might never have married but,
although she didn't feel inclined to ask for details of his conquests, he was skilled in the art of lovemaking and did not
disappoint.

For two whole weeks then, on honeymoon on a Greek island,
soaking up the sun with the man she loved at her side,
Francesca could acknowledge that at last after some tough
lonely years things were looking up. David thought it such a
novelty to have a wife and was boyishly thrilled when he introduced her as such. By then she was getting used to the
reaction, the surprised look, the nudges, and it did not help
that she looked considerably younger than her forty one years,
but she was too happy to care.

Let people think what they would.

For a brief time she was Mrs David Porter and, although she
worried a little about her new life up in the wilds of Yorkshire,
she was going to make it work. David had been used to getting
his own way for so long that it would take some time for her to
nudge him to her way of thinking.

She must be patient.

Returning from honeymoon, they got down to the serious job
of learning to live with each other, each of them long used to

the single life so that for both of them there were adjustments to be made. For two whole months then, busily making plans for their future together, Francesca was the happiest she had been in a long time. She no longer had a job and although she was aware that eventually she would have to face the thorny issue of getting another one without upsetting him, for the moment she was busy enough coping with the business of moving house and looking after her new husband.

Happiness though had proved an elusive thing and she might have known, knowing her luck that it would not last.

Chapter Three

SELINA'S HOME WITH its interior designer input was predictably eye-catching and a huge display of white lilies sat atop the hall table, the purity of white flowers being Selina's choice throughout the house. The tiled floor shone, courtesy of the cleaning lady, and on the wall there was a large gilt-framed traditional-type painting of a sunny country scene.

The children were out for a walk in the park with nanny and the house was unusually silent although one of the cats appeared at the head of the stairs to stare disdainfully down at them.

'I've put you in Bethany's room,' Selina announced, flinging her car keys unceremoniously on the polished table top before setting off up the stairs.

'Where have you put *her?*' Francesca asked with alarm, unhappy to be responsible for turfing the nanny out.

'We've cleared one of the attic rooms. She'll be fine up there. I've had to tell her why you're staying, Francesca, and she's very sympathetic. She's rather an emotional girl so whatever you do avoid eye contact or she'll dissolve.'

She could talk, Francesca thought.

The nanny's ex-room was big and comfortably furnished with an en-suite bathroom. It was at the rear of the house looking out onto the rough and tumble of the garden and as

Selina went back downstairs to make the coffee, Francesca put down her bags and crossed over to the window looking out on the murky late spring day. Early spring had come and gone before she had time to focus on it properly although she had a distant memory of spring flowers in the garden of the house that might have been theirs.

She could forget Yorkshire where she had left David. His ashes were scattered on Ilkey Moor as he wished and she was back to square one.

Single and a bit scared.

Selina was right of course. Her heart had never been in the move up there, but it had been David's dream and, because she loved him, she was prepared to go along with it. But being prepared to go along with it was not the same as being enthusiastic about it and would she ever have been happy up there? Would it have turned out to be an awful mistake? Would she have begun to resent him because of it? David had insisted she give up her job, a job she loved – fair enough because she could not continue it because of the distance – but he also expected her to more or less retire as he had retired and, although she had agreed to it, it might have been a sacrifice too many.

Looking back, looking at it with the benefit of hindsight, Francesca was not sure their marriage would have worked long term and more than anything that saddened her. It was not the age difference, she could cope with that, rather it was their different ideas, their different take on life and what was important to each of them. She had rushed into it despite this, because as she was not intending to have children, getting married had not been one of the key things on her agenda. She would in fact have been perfectly happy to conduct an affair with him in which they might each hang onto their single status, and she might keep her independence and her own place, but that did not wash with him.

She had been swayed a little by that powerful aphrodisiac that a man in David's position throws out, but she was not going to confess her doubts to anybody not even Selina, especially not her, and she knew she had to put that thought right out of her head because it would complicate matters and make the grieving process more difficult.

'I just hope you know what you're letting yourself in for,' Selina told her as she pinned a rose onto Francesca's dress on the morning of her wedding. 'He's a wonderful man – that goes without saying – but he's stubborn as hell. You should have dug your heels in, darling, about the Yorkshire thing. It's purely a whim. He'll miss London like hell and where will he get his suits and shirts from up there?'

'There are shops,' Francesca told her with a smile. 'And very good ones too in Leeds and Harrogate. I'm warming to it anyway. The moors remind me of Dartmoor and I don't believe he will miss London. I certainly won't. And we can always get the train down here, come down for lunch that sort of thing.'

'If you say so.' Selina stood back and eyed her critically, taking stock of her and then nodding with satisfaction. 'You look fabulous, darling. Sometimes I wish I was a brunette. Clients might take me more seriously if I didn't look quite so fluffy.'

It was a simple Register Office wedding and Francesca had opted for a peach-coloured dress with a flattering crossover bodice, hatless, her hair pinned up on top of her head as he liked it. David looked wonderful and when she made her vows with just a tearful Selina and Clive and another couple David knew in attendance, Francesca had truly believed she was doing the right thing.

But even before he died, doubts had begun to emerge.

She missed her father on her wedding day, the father who should have been escorting her proudly down the aisle – even though there was no such thing in a Register Office – but it would have been nice if he had been there on her big day.

She had informed her childhood friend Izzy via a text message – shame on her – that she had married and Izzy, bless her, sent her a congratulations card and an M&S voucher, but so far she had not told Izzy that she was a widow. Their correspondence over many years via Christmas and birthday cards continued in a dogged fashion interspersed with occasional phone calls and neither of them seemed able to shake it off, to sever the friendship completely even though Francesca had no intention of returning to Devon, not ever, and Izzy was still firmly entrenched there. Looking back, it seemed odd that she had been the one to move away, to go for the big London job because when they were young she would have banked on Izzy doing just that.

Francesca had sent congratulations cards and a small gift on the birth of each of Izzy's daughters and Izzy would stick a photograph of the new addition in a card, but it remained and was likely to remain purely a long-distance friendship.

When she informed Izzy she was married she had been short with details and had not mentioned his age for it bothered her a little what Izzy might think, although she was confident that if Izzy was to meet David he would charm her worries away. What would David have made of Izzy? In private he would probably have considered her to be just a little too exuberant, verging on the slightly vulgar with her bright laugh and voluptuous figure. She would, she realized, have defended Izzy to the last for she owed her so much and she must never forget that.

Under the circumstances, perhaps it was just as well that they would never meet.

At eighteen, Francesca was delighted and relieved to get the grades required for her university course up in Aberdeen, finally able to go off to college and escape her mother's martyrdom. In her second term up there, with no consultation her mother had upped and left the old house, sold it off, and settled in Kent buying a small flat and advising Francesca in one of her rare communications that she had found it necessary to get rid of most of her stuff because there was no room for it in the new place. And by the way she could put her up on a sofa bed in the lounge should she choose to visit.

With an invitation as lukewarm as that, Francesca did not bother.

Her mother did not shut her out completely, but very nearly, even avoiding the trip up to Francesca's graduation pleading it was too far to travel. She felt her mother's absence keenly when she saw all the other new graduates having photographs taken with their families. And the final insult was that her mother refused to let anyone tell her when she was near death so that she knew nothing about it until it was over.

The unpalatable truth was that her mother never forgave her for what happened to her brother James. She carried that bitterness and resentment deep inside her like a hard stone until the day she died.

Izzy was the one cheerful link to the past, the one person with whom she shared the secret of what had really happened on the day of James's accident and Francesca found she was oddly moved by the M&S voucher and the wedding congratulations card with the 'About bloody time' message scrawled on it.

And now Izzy would never meet David and be at the receiving end of his charm.

Francesca knew that many of David's colleagues missed out on the charm and thought him grumpy, but it was an aspect of his personality that amused her. The sex was fine, not the mind-boggling variety she had experienced occasionally when younger, but fine, and it wasn't until a couple of months into the marriage that his stubbornness had begun to grate on her. David was always right even when he was patently wrong and she guessed that in his profession that would have been a serious handicap.

She was not somebody standing in the dock.

She was his wife.

It wouldn't have been long before she started to question him.

It wouldn't have been long before she started to argue with him.

All the conversations they had had were now mere memories and she found herself frequently recalling them word for word as a sort of comfort.

'I don't want to live anywhere too remote,' she had said as they sat relaxing in the sitting room of his tall narrow town house. It was a cluttered house, if you can refer to precious antiques and bric-a-brac as clutter, but she was working on it, determined on a fresh start once they moved into the new house.

'Of course not. We shall make sure you are within easy reach of Harrogate and Leeds,' he said, eyes twinkling. 'Can't have you too far from the shops, can we?'

'It's not just that,' she told him a little impatiently because when it came to shopping she was no Selina. 'I need company. People to talk to.'

Trying hard because she was not a natural in the kitchen, she recalled she had cooked a pretty good meal that evening with David passing on the cheese course because of concerns over levels of fat. After the meal which they ate in the splendour of the dining-room he had removed himself from the table, taking his glass of wine with him, and making no effort to help with the clearing-up. Francesca, muttering, dumped everything, china included, loudly and carelessly into the dishwasher before joining him. He was puffing on his cigar and sitting in his favourite armchair. It was a horrible chair, high backed, covered in crimson velvet and one thing was sure, antique or not, it was not making the trip up to Yorkshire. She might have to bribe the removal people to 'lose' it in transit but she would worry about that when the time came.

She loved him, how she loved him and yet she was beginning to understand the doubts that people had expressed about the wisdom of marrying a long-time bachelor and she knew it would be an uphill struggle for David to learn to share his life with anybody, even her.

Sitting opposite him that evening, biting her tongue to stop a sarcastic remark about the lack of help he had given her in the kitchen, she saw the bundle of estate agent particulars sitting on the low table and realized that his mind was set on Yorkshire and she might as well get used to it. However, she was not giving up without a fight and she did not want to find herself living in the back of beyond. Picking up the notes on a newly refurbished former rectory, she reiterated that she really did not want to live anywhere too far removed from civilization.

'How many times do I have to tell you, you are not to worry about that,' he said. 'Life's different in the countryside,' he added with a smile she did not return because she felt he was humouring her. What did David know about the countryside? He may have been born and brought up in Yorkshire but he had lived in London for ages. 'In fact there is an awful lot going on there. I have a lot of contacts up there already and they are all most anxious to meet you, my darling.'

Contacts? Not friends?

'We can always join things.' He finished airily and they exchanged a small smile at that for they were neither of them great 'joiners-in'.

'I was brought up in Devon,' she reminded him. 'I do know about country life.'

'Devon!' he almost huffed the word. 'It's not the same thing at all, darling. You'll love the Dales.'

She relaxed a little, sharing his smile. Yes, she was sure she would.

'At least we won't have to worry about schools,' he went on, watching her as she thumbed through the various particulars they had collected. 'Selina tells me it's a considerable worry.'

'It's a nightmare. She's hyper-ventilating already and the boys are only at the nursery stage.'

'Do you regret not having children?' he asked, lowering his voice and surveying her in that way of his. 'I know we agreed not to bother trying, but it's not too late if you really …'

'No.' She waved an agitated hand.

'Thank God.' His relief was plain to see. 'You would have been an excellent mother though. Better than Selina I dare say.'

'How can you say that? She's a very good mother,' she said. 'I have no idea how she does it all.'

'She's a remarkable woman although she's a bit too emotional for my taste. She has trouble staying detached and in our profession that's an essential. There's no room for sentiment. The golden rule is never to get involved personally.'

Francesca smiled. Nobody could accuse David of being over-emotional and she recalled Selina telling her that on one occasion a grateful client had thrown her arms round him and she had seen him recoil in horror.

'Now …' he said, returning to the matter in hand. 'Before we get up there we need to be absolutely sure about what we are looking for. Have you given it any more thought? We shall need five bedrooms.'

'Why so many?' She frowned at him. 'We'll never fill five bedrooms.'

'It's a matter of proportion. A five bedroom house will give us the space we need elsewhere,' he said, using the persuasive voice he probably used on nervous witnesses. 'I know a lot of people up there and I have certain standards to keep up. I expect we shall do a lot of entertaining once we get settled in. I want to show you off, darling, and you have nothing to fear. You are a good cook although if you prefer we can always call on caterers. That's what I used to do when I was on my own.'

'There's no need for that now,' she told him with more confidence than she felt. Cooking was a doddle, Selina had assured her, if you followed a recipe to the death and avoided experimenting.

'I've drawn up a list of must-haves,' he continued. 'A criteria of essentials. You must do one too and then we'll see where we need to compromise.'

That sounded ominous, but compromise had to work both ways and she was quietly determined he was not going to get all his own way.

In the event, he did get his own way and the house they settled for was a beautiful if slightly dilapidated affair, a touch too big, a touch too far out of Harrogate for her liking, but she was promised a new little car and although she felt she had capitulated just a little too easily, that she had sold out in a big way, she wanted it to work.

How she wanted it to work.

As it happened, they never got round to signing the contract and the vendors, after thinking they had a sale at long last, must have been furious. Honestly, the lengths some people would go to in order to avoid the final signature.

Dying of all things.

In the nanny's former room in Selina's house, Francesca checked her appearance in the mirror and managed a rueful smile, making her way downstairs to the kitchen as she heard Selina yell that coffee was ready. She took in the mess that was the family kitchen/diner and knew that she could not stay here for very long. It was not fair to Selina or her husband for them to suffer the embarrassment of having a bereaved widow in tow, having to shush the children for fear of upsetting her, not quite sure how much to mention David in her presence. She would keep right on smiling, but she knew that they were all watchful and wondering when the smiling would cease.

She must do something.

But, just now, she had no idea what.

Chapter Four

MONEY THANKFULLY WAS not a problem.

When they married, David rushed to make a will surprising her that a man in his position had not done so earlier. He was keeping it simple and leaving her the lot but would she make sure that his two favourite charities received a goodly chunk. Aside from the paintings, David had built up an impressive portfolio of funds, had investments galore and it was no secret, to her and to others that she had become a lady of some considerable means.

She felt a little like a character in a Jane Austen novel. If that were so then suitors, some dreadfully *un*suitable, would be buzzing around before long. Selina had hinted at this, telling her to watch her back while she was vulnerable. Word had got round, she said, that David had left behind a young beautiful widow and some men might wish to try their luck.

Francesca had laughed at that for she was neither particularly young nor beautiful, but she knew that, as ever, Selina was just trying to cheer her up. She also suggested that Francesca might go travelling, shoot off to warm foreign climes and relax under a hot sun but that felt like running away and without David it would not be the least enjoyable.

She much preferred to stick it out here on familiar territory and work things through in her own way.

She could if she wanted become a lady of leisure.

She did not.

'Where's *your* daddy?' Cosmo asked as she closed the book at bedtime.

Francesca smiled, ruffling his blond hair and helping him to snuggle down under his Thomas the Tank Engine quilt.

'Where's *your* daddy?' he repeated.

She could not answer his question for if she went for the real daddy option then she had no idea where her father was and, if Cosmo meant David which he might well do she did not feel like going down the gone to heaven route just now. In any case, the little boy was sleepy, having trouble keeping his eyes open, such blue eyes just like his mother's. 'Mummy will be in to see you in a minute,' she whispered, neatly side-stepping the question. 'Sweet dreams. Good night, lovey.' She leaned down to kiss his chubby little cheek. He smelled of newly bathed child, a unique aroma, and somewhere deep down her maternal genes stirred just a little.

Bethany was bathing baby Charles and, contrary to Selina's protestations that he never had the time Clive was reading to his eldest son in his bedroom. Selina was downstairs ranting on the phone to one of her work colleagues, a subordinate by the sound of it, annoyed to have been rung at home just at the crucial bedtime hour and Francesca and Cosmo were alone in the lovely room that was his. He was a lucky child. He had everything a little boy could wish for in this large playroom cum bedroom, and just for a moment as she waited just inside the door to make sure he was settling, Francesca was reminded of her brother James and how she had sometimes read to him when he was small. She had never needed to explain to James where his daddy was because James had never known him and now, as then, she found herself buckling under the puzzlement and disappointment that her father's sudden disappearance had brought about.

Something terrible had happened and her little girl head had sensed it hearing whispered conversations that were shut off immediately she appeared. She did not remember significant rows or raised voices, rather an atmosphere following James's arrival that for a while she had put down to the difficulties of his birth and her mother's subsequent ill-health. Her mother, for all her cheery outgoing personality, could have won an Oscar for sulking.

She remembered the last time she saw her father, how he had come up to her room and stood there a moment, searching inadequately for the right words and in the event not coming up with anything. However, as he left, he had hugged her so hard that she had squealed and said he was hurting her.

'Sorry, poppet. You are my clever girl, Frankie, and I want you to promise to be good for your mother. Look after her for me.'

It seemed a strange thing to say.

Without knowing, Cosmo had hit it on the head.

Where the hell *was* her daddy?

After a week at Selina's, it was becoming impossible. Clive was being incredibly patient with the situation but he always looked faintly surprised and awkward when they met up and she worried that, even though she stayed in her room in the evenings half heartedly watching television or listening to the radio she was intruding into his precious private time with his wife.

Francesca knew she would have to get things together. With her flat sold and David's house as near as sold, she had to find somewhere else to live. She was making life difficult for she would have been quite at liberty to withdraw his property from the sale and continue to live in it herself but she did not want to disappoint the family who were buying it as she had disappointed the lovely people at the house up in Yorkshire and it was just too big for her anyway. Selina wanted her to find a flat close by but, much as she liked Selina, Francesca knew that would be disastrous.

She was determined not to become an encumbrance.

She needed her independence.

She had lived alone before David and she would do so again and now she had money too so she could afford something really special. She started to put out feelers in an area close enough to Selina but not that close. Giving up her job might have been a mistake and Selina certainly seemed to think so but she did not feel she could go back. She had done the cut-throat business world to death, was guilty of turning a blind eye too often to the injustice of it all, had wrung her creative juices dry and she needed something less intense.

On the second Monday of her stay at Selina's, she went back to the house she still thought of as David's to pick up some boxes containing her personal things. The house was slowly losing heart, strangely echoey even though not all the furniture had gone. She was leaving the curtains – not her choice anyway – for the new people and, when they heard what had happened they came round to pay their respects and with a great deal of embarrassment made an offer for some of the things they would like to keep.

Locking up, she felt very little for the house, just a rather grand property that's all it was to her, and she would certainly shed no tears about leaving it for good.

However, her presence at Selina's was starting to cause complications and inconvenience. She felt, notwithstanding being a stand-in bedtime story reader, that she was in everybody's way, under everybody's feet, and there would be an uncomfortable silence when she appeared as people struggled to find the right words to say. Laughter was cut short as if they had no right to feel happy when, despite the front she put on, she was so sad. And, not least, poor Bethany was squashed into an attic room with hardly any space for her bits and bobs.

Waking up one morning and feeling suddenly more capable of sorting things out, Francesca assured Selina she would be out of her hair soon and even though Selina made all the right noises, insisting there was no hurry, Francesca recognized the signs of relief at the announcement. There were a couple of likely looking flats that she had made arrangements to view and Francesca was relieved too that the end was in sight.

But for the moment she was stuck with staying at Selina's for the next week or so and as she drove back there from David's house, Francesca reflected that she had done this particular trip so many times recently that the car very nearly knew the way itself. Arriving at a familiar important junction, she found that, through lack of attention she was in the wrong lane in very busy traffic. It would be awkward but not impossible to switch lanes, but instead she found herself anchored there, waiting patiently at the lights and firmly indicating right instead of left.

Heading due west.

She was not to know at the time but it was a decision that would change her life.

Chapter Five

FRANCESCA HAD NOT noticed the weather much since David died. It was strange how, after such an experience, such a shock, her mind had funnelled into itself. She found herself not caring about the international, national or even the local situation, tossing aside newspapers that she had previously perused vigorously. Whilst staying at Selina's, Clive, completely at sea as to how best to deal with her, had made valiant attempts to engage her in political debate but she had proved a sorry opponent, putting up no fight to challenge his views.

'You've disappointed him,' Selina told her with a smile. 'He likes a good old argument. That's why he liked David. David would always stand up to him even though he irritated the hell out of Clive because out of nowhere he would produce that final put-down to which there was no answer. He did the same thing in court of course and that's why he was so bloody brilliant.' The smile faded as she caught Francesca's expression. 'Oh sorry, darling, there I go again.'

'It's OK. You can talk about him.'

She was becoming fed up with Selina constantly back-tracking and apologizing. It was not Selina's fault for she was doing her best to keep everybody happy, but all that concerned Francesca was her own predicament and what was happening to her. She was doing her best to keep smiling at all costs so as

not to upset people around her but in private she found it difficult just now to rustle up the merest hint of a smile.

Grief makes you selfish.

It wraps round you like a cocoon, holding you fast at first,
and only gradually can you begin to reach outside it. It was the
little things that were slowly bringing her out of it, words and
actions poking through and forcing her to take notice, although
she was quick at first to retreat into the shell she had created.
The children had helped, too young to understand what was
happening but it was one of the cats who had taken it upon
itself to console, coming uninvited into her bedroom where she
would find it asleep in the morning, leaping onto her lap during
the day where she would find herself stroking its soft grey fur.

It was odd she should find it such a comfort because she was
not a cat person, but Sheba the cat obviously thought otherwise.

Wise creature.

As she drove west out of London, she could physically feel
something lifting from her and it came as a surprise to find
she was humming along to a tune on the radio.

Well, well.

It had been a dull start to the day, but the clouds were beginning to disperse and the sun was doing its best to make an
impression. As it did so, she felt her spirits lifting and some of
the grief escaping as if through a pin hole. Strangely content,
she drove on, stopping at one point for petrol when it would
have been possible to abort the journey and return to Selina's
but instead she continued steadily on her way. She stopped
later at a roadside café for a meal, surprised at how hungry
she was and choosing the 'All Day Breakfast' option which
involved stuffing herself with bacon, eggs, sausages and the
like. In the Ladies, she dug out lipstick and scent and fluffed up

her hair, smiling inanely at herself in the mirror because there was nobody else around and deciding that, all in all, she wasn't looking too bad.

She had passed the 'Welcome to Devon' sign and was indicating her intention to turn off the main road before she had time to think about it, driving more slowly through several villages, very nearly pulling over at a farm that advertised cream teas but, on top of the big breakfast that seemed just a few calories too many. On either side of the road the moor stretched out, uneven ground with the Tors pushing up in the distance. It had been so long since she was here and, opening the window, she felt the fresh sweet air rush in, bringing with it a memory of brisk walks over the gorse-strewn ground, the springy turf dotted with sheep and ponies. Sometimes, back in the good days, long before James was on the scene, her mother would abandon her work for the day and they would head off up the lane from their house, over the cattle grid and onto the moor. For ten years it was often just the two of them, her dad at school, her mum giving herself time off from her creative schemes and Francesca never minded that she was an only child, enjoyed it in fact.

Those were the days when her dad was always around and although she never attended the private school at which he taught – her mother thought it a bad idea – she and her mother often went along to the various events there. She remembered that her mother never looked like any of the other mothers in her flowing skirts and crazy patchwork jacket, but her magnificent red hair meant she was noticed.

'This is Francesca,' her mother would say when somebody enquired. 'She's like her father,' she would add, seeming to Francesca to be apologizing because her daughter had not inherited her fabulous foxy mane.

'Mr Blackwell is a delightful man,' the person would go on to say. 'Quite absorbed in his work of course. Wrapped up in the past shall we say?'

It was a put-down.

Francesca was too young to understand that but she did not fail to notice how irritated her mother became at these events. On the way home on one occasion her mother referred to the school mothers as snotty madams and her father had laughed and said that snotty or not they carried an awful lot of weight and it was wise to stay on the right side of them. They were full of their own importance, he said, and when they worked together on a pet project they were a formidable team. The headmaster was terrified of them because he knew that, if he put a foot wrong, they would have him booted out in no time.

'You cross those ladies at your peril,' he had said.

It wasn't until thirty odd years later that Francesca understood exactly what that meant.

Why did he leave his job and his family so abruptly?

Why did he never ever make contact again?

It was James's arrival that sparked it off and even prior to his birth she had begun to notice a change in her father. In later life, trying to make some sense of it, it occurred that perhaps James was not her father's child, that maybe her mother, her vivacious red-haired mother, had had an affair and that her father had been unable to cope with that. They seemed an odd couple; her father an earnest softly spoken man, her mother a shining effervescent beacon who lit up a room the moment she entered it.

So her parents were incompatible and the marriage had probably run its course but that was no excuse for abandoning *Francesca*.

You only had to look at Francesca to know that she was her father's daughter. She had his colouring, his eyes, his shy smile, a habit of tilting her head at a certain angle when she was thinking. You had to look carefully to see anything of her mother.

Aged ten and a bit, she gained a brother and lost a father.

When her brother James was very small, she and her mother used to take one of his hands each and swing him up high whereupon he would giggle with delight and say 'again'. One, two three … swing him high!

The ten year age gap was too big for Francesca to feel entirely comfortable with childish games but part of her enjoyed it too and that was enough to squash the rebellious streak. By the time she was fourteen, James was a hefty four-year-old and far too big for such things. He was a bright happy child, not seeming to miss a male influence in his life, chatty and naughty, a joy and a mischief in equal measures.

On those days, during the long summer holidays, her mother would assemble a picnic of sorts although, as often as not, when they arrived there would be little pots of trifle but no spoons and she would have failed to put the lid back properly on the jar of pickled onions – she adored them – and the sandwiches and butterfly cakes would be soggy and vinegary. 'Who cares? It all gets mixed up inside. Eat it, Francesca, and stop fussing.'

Her mother called her Francesca, her father too although sometimes he would abbreviate it to Frankie which James picked up on but she herself liked the full title because she thought Francesca sounded slightly foreign and interesting. Her mother had a thing about names. She was Amanda and woe betide anybody who tried to call her Mandy.

It was her mother's laugh she remembered, a hoarse throaty

laugh that was seldom heard afterwards. Her mother was an eccentric – did not care what people thought of her – arty, her hair a mass of rich red curls that Francesca thanked heaven she had not inherited; her fingernails were always sticky with the clay of her beloved pots.

James was a typical boy, forever in trouble. Once he got his little legs stuck half-way across the cattle grid, too impatient to use the gate at the side, so that her mother had to struggle over to rescue him, pink cheeked and cursing, scooping him up and having a fit of giggles as they climbed out.

'I'll swing for you, young man,' she had said. 'Just look at your shoes.'

Francesca watched from the safety of the lane, her feet primly on solid ground, her shoes un-scuffed, feeling that touch of jealousy stabbing at her because, whatever she might say, however she might deny it, James with his red hair was her mother's favourite child and his arrival had deprived her of that special dubious pleasure of being the only one.

Prior to his arrival, preparations began in earnest. The nursery was decorated in bright sunshine yellow, baby clothes started to appear and her mother let Francesca hold her hand over her tummy to feel the baby as it moved about.

The first time she felt it, she jerked her hand back, shocked at the force of the movement.

'He kicked me.'

'He's just saying hello to his big sister,' her mother said with a smile.

She supposed she blamed James later for making her mother so ill. He came early and she saw him in the incubator at the hospital and he was every bit as small as the dolls she still secretly played with but his head was bigger. She was allowed to hold him when he came home, but he was still very small and floppy and her mother hovered anxiously until she handed him back. He stiffened in Francesca's arms, looked anxious himself as if he knew she didn't have a clue what she was doing.

Francesca knew that his needs had to come first, but she could not help the resentment nibbling at her, the irritation that she had to do so much of the work herself round the house because her mother took some time to recover from her ordeal.

'Never again,' she heard her say to a neighbour when Francesca was not supposed to be listening. 'He's the last one. It was horrendous. I thought I was going to die. I lost half of my blood.'

Francesca crept away before she could be accused of listening in, wondering just how much blood that was. She asked her dad how many pints of blood you had in your body and he said he thought it was eight, but he could be wrong and why did she want to know?

With her mother not recovered fully for some time, her dad did his bit round the house in his clumsy fashion although he took his job at school seriously and, if he came home early, he always brought work home with him. Gradually Francesca learned not to be quite so worried about handling James, managing it eventually with a degree of competence although you wouldn't have thought so because James still seemed suspicious of her.

Things had changed so much with his arrival that for a while she forgot about the strained atmosphere that still existed. The realization came as she noted the difference in the relationship between her parents and Izzy's. There was a lot of cheery shouting and laughter at Izzy's house, secret smiles shared between her mum and dad, something that was singularly absent in hers.

She tried to ignore it and to their credit they each tried not to let it disturb her, but instinctively she knew something was wrong and then, one day, without a word he was gone. His boots were gone from the porch, his coat was gone from the peg in the hall and upstairs all his stuff had disappeared from the bathroom.

In the sitting-room, half of the books on the shelves were gone too.

'Where has daddy gone?'

'It's complicated. I'll explain when you're older,' her mother said and never did. None of Francesca's questions were ever answered, her mother seeming to have put it out of her head, obsessed as she was with the baby.

When James was a little bit bigger and starting to recognize them and smile, a more interesting stage, she brought her best friend Izzy round to see him. Her mother did not care for Izzy, thought her too familiar and too forward although she would not explain to Francesca what she meant by that. She did not care for Izzy's mother either, but there the feeling was mutual. With her plummy voice and total disregard for the locals as she called them her mother was given a wide berth by most of them. They had tried to entice her into the community but her pointblank refusal to join in anything meant that they no longer bothered to try.

This all went over Izzy's head. Izzy, maternal to the core, went completely daft about the baby, imploring her mother to let her hold him and then picking him up and nestling him immediately to her chest as if it was the most natural thing in the world.

'Hello, baby,' she murmured, stroking his cheek.

James went quiet at that, hooked his hand round her little finger and did not wriggle as he did when Francesca picked him up.

'He feels safe with you,' her mother said to Izzy with some surprise, glancing at Francesca but blessedly not stating the obvious and saying that, even though she was his sister, he felt nervous in *her* arms.

And, in view of what was to happen later, he was quite right to be so.

Chapter Six

FRANCESCA SIGHED, PULLING off the road at a lay-by.

Maybe James had known then, even as a baby, that, when push came to shove, she would let him down. Izzy had come into her own on that day and what happened had bound them together, Izzy insisting that it really was not Francesca's fault and she must not blame herself.

If only her mother had thought the same.

Izzy, the very soul of discretion, had kept her mouth shut and even though for a while Francesca was not entirely sure if she could trust her, she soon realized that Izzy was keeping the episode firmly to herself to the extent of not even telling her own mother the truth.

'Well done, Francesca,' Izzy's plump cheerful mother had said, pulling her close and hugging her. 'You did your best. You couldn't have done more for him.'

But it was far worse when the local paper got wind of it and the reporter came along, notebook as well as camera in hand because they didn't run to having a photographer too.

'Put your arms round each other,' she instructed Francesca and Izzy and awkwardly they tried to pose for her. 'Don't look so serious,' she told them. 'You can manage a little smile between you, can't you?'

She had to be joking?

Wishing she hadn't dragged all that up again in her head, Francesca reached for her phone, saw that at last she had a good signal and rang Selina.

It was answered at the second ring.

'Where the hell are you? We've been worried sick, darling. You haven't been picking up. Did you get my message?'

'The reception is a bit off. Sorry, I didn't mean to worry you. I'm in Devon.'

'Devon? As in Devon and Cornwall?'

'Of course. Is there any other?'

'What on earth are you doing there?'

She talked as if Francesca had landed on the moon.

'I come from Devon. Remember?'

'But we've an appointment to view a flat tomorrow morning. I was coming with you.'

'I'll cancel. There will be other flats.'

'Honestly, Francesca.' Exasperation flooded her voice. 'What's got into you?'

'I just needed to take a walk down memory lane. I did it on impulse.'

'On impulse? You drove over *two hundred miles* on impulse? That is a crazy idea.'

'Why?' She felt her hackles rising. 'Will you please stop telling me what to do? It feels good to be back.'

'For God's sake, Francesca, didn't you stop to think that we would be worried about you? I thought you might have had an accident. If you hadn't called by this evening I was seriously considering calling the police and reporting you missing.'

Francesca laughed at the indignation in her voice. 'For

heaven's sake, there's no need for such drama. I'm a grown woman, remember?'

'You are not acting like one. I am telling you I can do without this today.' Her sigh was deeply felt. 'It's been one of those awful days we dread. There's been an incident at nursery.'

'What's happened?'

'I was called in. I was just about to go into a meeting at work so it was hellish inconvenient but when you get summoned to attend by Miss Martin you drop everything. It turns out that Crispin was in a fight and had punched George who had banged his head so he had to be checked out at hospital just in case because they are scared shitless about liability issues.'

'Is he OK?'

'Absolutely fine. A little bump that's all, but she made me feel as if I was in the dock. Dreadful woman. However, I have to say that, on the evidence presented it doesn't look as if we have a leg to stand on. I could plead deliberate provocation because George has a distinctly sneaky look about him but you know what a little devil Crispin can be when he's roused. Just like his daddy. Anyway, there's been hell to pay. His mummy was called in too and she was not in a forgiving mood. I thought for a minute she was going to sue. In the end I smoothed things over by promising a huge donation to the summer raffle which she is in the process of organizing. It was bribery, darling, pure and simple.'

'Oh for goodness sake, Selina.'

'Exactly. Miss Martin kept the two of us waiting outside her office for ten minutes before she called us in. By that time I was ready to wring her neck. It was much ado about nothing. I've had to calm all sorts of ruffled feathers including Miss Martin who takes it all very seriously and then, when I finally got home feeling like a wet rag I find that you're not there and nobody knows where you are. Bethany is at her wits' end and convinced you've flipped and are lying dead in a ditch somewhere.'

'Will you calm down? I have not disappeared. I'm in Devon and I'm perfectly all right.'

'Are you quite sure about that? After all, you are in a vulnerable state just now. I can't believe the number of times I've had to repeat a question two or three times before you answer. You don't seem to be able to concentrate and I'm not sure you should be driving.'

'You know me better than that.' Francesca bit her lip, feeling guilty now to have worried her so. 'I do concentrate when I'm driving,' she went on firmly although she was aware that was not quite true. 'Nor am I suicidal. I'm going to get through this, but on my own terms if you will let me.'

'I know that, but I can't help worrying about you. You haven't let go yet. It's all bottled up and it's not good for you. You should have a good cry and you'll feel heaps better.'

'Stop it, Selina. It's the way I am. We bottle things up in our family.'

'David would have wanted me to keep an eye on you and I do feel sort of responsible,' Selina went on. 'After all, if I hadn't introduced you in the first place, you would have been spared all this.'

'Don't. You are being ridiculous. I wouldn't have missed knowing him for anything. They were very precious months we had together. I had hoped for longer but it wasn't to be.'

'Oh, Francesca ...' Selina was losing it, her voice catching.

Here we go again, thought Francesca, why is it that she, the bereaved widow, always ended up doing the consoling where Selina was concerned?

'You mustn't blame yourself, Selina. These things happen

and we can't do a thing about them,' she said, knowing it was a stupid thing to say, but it was sometimes better with Selina to keep it simple as she tended to over-analyse every situation. 'Look, you've had a bad day with Crispin and everything. Why don't you sit down and pour yourself a large gin and tonic? Bethany will look after the boys.'

'I have a drink in my hand as we speak. I am trying to be calm but I can't help thinking how I would feel if Clive suddenly dropped dead of a heart attack. I would go to pieces completely. And to find him dead in the chair as you did must have been horrific. I shook Clive awake the other evening when he was dozing off. I imagined for a minute he wasn't breathing. He was bloody annoyed I can tell you.'

Francesca held back a feeling of irritation.

'I'm sorry to have worried you,' she said. 'I should have rung before but there was a problem with my phone.' This was not entirely true and it was a lame excuse at best but she needed to make a token effort. 'It was very kind of you to offer to put me up and I am grateful. Please give my love to Clive and thank him for being so nice and tell the boys that I'll see them soon. You've been a real friend, but it's time Bethany had her room back. The poor girl's been very patient.'

'Eh, stop all that nonsense.' Selina laughed. 'You're very welcome and you know it. Are you quite sure you're all right? I don't like the idea of your being alone. What are you going to do? Are you coming back tomorrow? Where will you be staying tonight?'

'I could bunk down in the car, but on the other hand I do believe there are pubs and guest houses around here or I might even go the whole hog, blow the expense and stay in a hotel.'

'Don't be sarcastic, darling, it doesn't suit you. I didn't

imagine for one moment you would be pitching a tent some-where. But you can't just disappear, not now. What about the house? Don't you have things to do? When will you be back? Do you want me to cancel the appointment tomorrow?'

'Would you? Thanks, Selena. I don't know when I'll see you, but I'll keep in touch.'

She put the mobile phone back in her bag and considered what to do next. It was mid-afternoon and the moor beckoned and the heady scents of this tricky in-between season rushed in through the window. She took a deep breath and decided she needed a walk.

As well as the gorse with its custard yellow blossom, the bracken was stirring, unfolding together with a whole array of wild spring flowers. Wearing unsuitable footwear, Francesca tramped along a worn grassy path leaving the road and the car far behind and, as she did so, stopping to take it all in, to simply look at the vast emptiness of it all, she felt like a child again, half expecting to see her mother and James forging on into the distance, herself trailing behind.

'Come on, Francesca, get a move on.'

She had always been one step behind.

This wild place could change in the blink of an eye. She remembered cold February days, incessant rain making the grass moist and springy, low heavy swirling mist so specific to the moor which, if it thickened, quickly became disorientating. Boggy ground, fast-flowing streams and mist so thick it clings to you are the stuff of nightmares, but also a feature of this wonderful, wild, inspiring place.

There was no danger of that today. Today, she could see clearly for miles, her city lifestyle telling against her as she laboured steadily uphill until, pausing to catch her breath, she felt the tears bubbling up and before she knew it they were upon her, turned on like a tap, uncontrollable, grief-laden angry tears.

Tears for David or even her mother or James or maybe for her father, long gone but never forgotten.

Her mother, buttoned up emotionally, would not approve of tears and true to form, Francesca had not cried when she found David dead in the chair. She had not cried when she lay alone in the big bed they had so briefly shared. She had not cried when, accompanied by a pale and tearful Selina, she visited the registrars to record his death. She had not cried at the funeral either fuelling the feeling no doubt amongst some of his friends that her motives for marrying him had been dubious. She overheard somebody say that he was perfectly all right until he got married as if she was somehow responsible. She heard somebody else querying the choice of music.

Until she came along David had been alone in the world so she was not sure if anybody was there in the capacity of a true mourner. Somebody, one of his colleagues with a perfectly pitched courtroom voice, had read the beautiful Christina Rossetti's poem "Remember" and even then, firmly closeted in the front pew with Selina beside her holding her hand, Francesca focussed on the vicar's funereal face and did not cry.

Selina had done her best playing the part of bereaved best friend, a vision in a black dress emerging from church red-eyed giving Francesca a hug, but being too choked to speak coherently. Clive was beside her, looking suitably chastened although Francesca had caught him glancing at his watch – an unexpected funeral interrupting his highly organized work schedule.

'Look after her, Clive,' she had said, pushing a suddenly sobbing Selina towards his comforting arms.

Even when she was at last alone, when the funeral party was ended, Francesca still could not rustle up tears.

And now, unexpectedly, here they were.

She howled. She could not stop the sound escaping and it was frightening because she could not recall crying like this since she was a little girl. She had no tissues on her and all she could do was wipe away the tears with her hand, tasting the saltiness as liquid escaped onto her lips, her hand shaking with the shuddering breaths.

Thank heavens there was nobody about.

'David, you bloody fool,' she said aloud. 'What did you go and do that for? How could you? What am I going to do without you?'

She stumbled on unsteady feet and a sheep with a blue mark on its back crossed her path, pausing for a moment to glance at her before calling urgently for its lamb.

Giving a gigantic unladylike sniff, Francesca walked briskly back to the car.

She was home before she knew it.

Home?

It felt like it. Pulling to a halt in a car park by the river, Francesca was relieved to find it looked much the same. After nearly twenty five years, it looked much the same. Stepping out of the car as a nearby coach disgorged its excited passengers, Francesca felt she ought to point out to them that she was not just a casual visitor, but was born here, grew up here, that she had some claim to this town, this delightful historic town that was not merely a good stopping off point for them, a toilet and coffee break, before they continued west to Cornwall.

Watching them obediently following the signs to the 'town centre', Francesca took the other exit steps leading to the river walk. After a wet winter and weeks of spring rain, water was gushing down the weir, their mini Niagara, a solitary bewildered duck bobbing about until it reached the sudden calm of down-stream.

She was drenched herself for a moment in a sharp painful memory, thinking of all the times she had walked this very path with Izzy on their way home from school and it took a moment before she got her act together and headed into town. She must keep herself in check for she did not want a repeat performance of what had happened on the moor.

She did not expect to recognize anybody nor would anybody recognize her. Izzy had moved, along with her family, and now lived over in the South Hams near Kingsbridge so perhaps she should give her a call, arrange to meet half-way somewhere. Perhaps not. She was not sure she wanted to catch up with a mum of four; Francesca was a little worried by the prospect of how she might have changed, become middle-aged, although it was difficult to think of Izzy as that. She was sure Izzy of all people would be sympathetic to her needs just now and provide a good motherly shoulder to cry on, her sympathy would also be genuine: Izzy would understand how she felt in a way that Selina, for all her good intentions, never would.

She ought to get in touch, she owed it to Izzy, dearest Izzy, to get in touch but it would depend how long she stayed around. There was also the can of worms thing, the concern that she would be resurrecting the past and opening old wounds, old memories that they both wanted to forget.

Her feet carried her on a pedestrian auto-pilot past the bustling pannier market along the main street thronged with people enjoying the sunshine then up a little cobbled passageway in the direction of her old home, Lilac House. It would take ten minutes or so. It was steep, steep enough to need a helping iron handrail at one point and, out of condition as she was, she was puffing by the time she neared the top of the hill where it levelled out and there at last was the house. The beech hedge was neatly trimmed and a freshly mown-grass smell drifted over so at least it was being kept in good order. Francesca paused by the hedge, reluctant to go any further.

Why was she here and what on earth was she thinking of? She should abandon this stupid game now before it was too late, just go back to the car and drive off.

Anxiety and indecision made her sway on her feet and then something made her move forward and as the hedge ended and the gate emerged, she saw that not only was the house looking in excellent shape, it was also a B&B.

Chapter Seven

LILAC HOUSE WAS a wonderfully symmetrical house set well back from the lane. Beyond it, there were no more houses and the lane petered out eventually leading up to the cattle grid and the moor itself.

Not surprisingly, after all this time, the garden looked different, laid out now in a much more formal way and it had a welcoming look to it, the outside cared for and loved. There were several hanging baskets suspended from black chains along the front of the house. Francesca presumed that the beautiful clematis and jasmine plants that used to clamber in a delightful jumble above the porch later in the year were long gone but she hoped that they had been replaced with something similar. Her mother had been the gardener although she had loved the garden in a much more haphazard natural state and had been happy for weeds to compete for attention with more respectable flowers.

What would she make of this? This planted out perfection?

Francesca was up the path and into the front porch before she could change her mind. The open sided porch had a shiny red-tiled floor with a big umbrella container tucked in a corner and a vision of their family clutter, a jumble of outdoor shoes and Wellington boots flashed into her head as she rang the bell, hearing its melodic tune before a figure appeared behind the glass and the door opened.

'Good afternoon. Lovely to see you. You must be Miss Wetherall.'

He was wearing crumpled cargo shorts, army green, and a grubby white tee shirt, not a great look, but nevertheless he was an attractive looking man, in his early forties she supposed. His hair, she noted, needed a trim. It was the sort of dirty blond hair that is much more attractive on the male sex – a female would opt for highlights – and he was barefoot with tanned legs, an extremely easy-going look and she would not have been surprised if he spoke with an Australian accent.

'Sorry about this,' he said, interpreting her glance correctly and frowning down at his clothes. 'I was expecting you a little later, but it's not a problem. The room's ready for you. Come on in and welcome to Lilac House,' he added, standing aside and smiling.

'No, no, you misunderstand ... sorry, I'm not Miss Wetherall. I haven't booked in,' she said quickly, flashing an apologetic smile and feeling flustered now at her impulsiveness. 'I'm just in the area for a short time. I don't suppose you have a room by any chance? Oh sorry again ...' she added, catching sight of the 'NO VACANCIES' sign in the window. 'Obviously not.'

'Oh, that.' He followed her glance. 'I've been working flat out all morning and I haven't got round to switching it round. As it happens, you're in luck. We've had a cancellation. The Poppy room is our smallest room, up in the gods I'm afraid, and it does share a bathroom with the other attic room so it's not ideal.'

She smiled, amused at his negative selling technique. How not to sell a room, she thought, her business instincts kicking in.

'Would you like me to show it to you before you decide?' He whipped up a leaflet that was lying on a side table. 'Terms as set out,' he said briskly. 'If you are happy with that and like the room, I can show you up straightaway and get you booked in.'

'I'm sure the room will be lovely and I really don't mind sharing a bathroom for a couple of nights,' Francesca said, determined now to stay. The man introduced himself as Gareth before excusing himself, leaving her to browse through the little tourist leaflets on the table. He reappeared moments later with his hair combed wearing a clean tee-shirt and with sandals on, and as he fussed around with her credit card and the booking in slip, she very nearly blurted out that she had once lived here, years ago, and was dying to see what he had done to it.

The hall, square with rooms leading off, looked very smart – probably having been recently decorated in anticipation of the busy summer season. The original tiled floor was no longer visible covered with a plain cream carpet. A big glass vase of flowers artfully arranged caught her eye, a far cry indeed from her mother's much more natural approach. Her mother's creative eye preferred bunches of flowers from the garden stuffed into all sorts of weird and wonderful containers sometimes of her own making, anything but a traditional glass vase.

After the preliminaries, Francesca followed him upstairs, pausing at the window on the half-landing to stare out. The lay-out was much the same in the back garden as she remembered – free and easy, stopping just short of what could be called overgrown. Perhaps misinterpreting her silence for disapproval, Gareth said they had a man who did the gardening, but his wife was ill so things had got a bit behind. He was doing the front garden himself, but mowing the lawn and trimming the hedge was about the extent of his expertise.

'It's charming,' she assured him, following him up the final flight.

The so called Poppy Room turned out to be one of the rooms they once used for storage crammed with all their overspill clobber, but it was now transformed. It was kitted out with nice quality furniture, good looking cream bed linen, fairly bland paintings of local scenes on the three plain walls, the wall behind the bed covered in striking poppy printed wallpaper with matching lightweight curtains. It was pretty but also unashamedly feminine.

'Happy with it?' He hovered, jingling a key as, for a moment, stunned by it, she was speechless.

'Absolutely. My bags are still in the car,' she explained. 'I'll go and bring the car round.'

'Yes, do that. Which car park are you in, Mrs Porter?'

'The one by the river.'

'Ah. It's a bit complicated getting back here by car. Let me see. If you ...'

'I know the way back here,' she interrupted him with a smile. 'Thank you.'

'Fine.' If he was surprised he did not show it. 'When you get here, if you drive past the house round the side there's plenty of room to park beside the—'

'The old stone garage?'

'Well, yes, you could call it that. It's used as the office just now.' Gareth smiled. 'Give me a shout if you need any help with the bags and then I'll make you a pot of tea. Would you like some scones? I've just made a fresh batch. In fact, I can do a Devon cream tea for you. Would you like that?'

My goodness, as well as having interesting green-grey eyes and a blitz of a smile, this man could make scones too. Noticing the quick glance he gave her, one of those indisputably male ones, Francesca found herself pushing at her hair in a gesture that used to please David, instantly annoyed that she should draw attention to herself. She knew her heavy silky hair to be one of her best features and she had worn it shoulder-length for years now, enjoying the variety of styles that could be achieved.

She set off to retrieve the car wondering as she sat inside and slotted the key into the ignition if she should just cut her losses and make a run for it. Having given out her card details, she would be charged for the room but so what? On reflection, she decided she could not do that to such a nice uncomplicated man as Gareth who would have the kettle on and the cream scones ready by now.

She could not possibly stand him up.

Gareth insisted on carrying her bags up to her room although she had left the boxes brought from David's old house in the boot of the car. She would have to return to London sooner rather than later, but it could wait a few days.

'Take your time,' Gareth said, putting her bags inside the door and handing her the key. 'Whenever you're ready come down to the sitting-room.'

Mindful that she would be sharing the bathroom with the as yet unseen Miss Rosemary Wetherall, Francesca washed and refreshed her make-up before going back downstairs and into the sitting-room.

'Oh, you've found it then,' Gareth said a moment later, popping his head round the door and seeming surprised to find her there. 'The dining-room's opposite.'

'I know.'

At that he gave her a quick puzzled glance before once more assuming the mantle of host. 'Give me a minute. It's all ready.'

'If you've time please join me,' she said, keen to talk to him before any other guests arrived.

The sitting room was light and airy with none of the claustrophobic feel she remembered, but then her mother had always favoured weighty dark curtains with under nets, too much dark wood furniture, a clutter of ornaments and busy wallpaper. She knew what she liked and would probably have been more at home in the Victorian age.

'You have a lovely house,' she said by way of a starting point when he was back with the refreshments. 'It's tucked away, isn't it?'

'You'd be surprised how many people who've lived here all their lives don't know of its existence. It's a secret house.'

'I suppose it's because the lane looks as if it just fades away,' she said. 'The last thing you expect to see is a house like this. How long have you been living here?'

'Oh I don't live here,' he explained, his easy smile rattling her a little. 'The Sandersons own it, but they are away and I'm acting as caretaker for them. I'm a friend of Pamela's and she knows I can rustle up a good breakfast so she roped me in for looking after things whilst they're on this around the world cruise. It is their fortieth wedding anniversary so it's been a dream for a long time.'

'You have a light touch,' she said, dabbing at her mouth with a napkin wondering when, if ever, she was going to break the news about her involvement with the house. 'Are you staying here then?'

'For the moment. Someone has to be here all the time or most of the time to take bookings, tidy up and cook the breakfasts and so on. I live in a caravan over in Cornwall near Tintagel. Once I'm there, a walk across the fields, down a path and I'm at this little beach with rock pools and a cove straight out of a kids' storybook. It's magical.'

'It sounds idyllic.'

'You could say that.'

'You are not a Cornish man though?'

'How did you guess?' he grinned. 'No, I'm from the London area. I worked in the city for years and then one day ...' he paused. 'Sorry, I don't want to bore you.'

'You won't,' she said with a smile, surprised at the sudden flow of information from him. 'I think I can guess anyway. One day you woke up and asked yourself what's it all about? So you handed in your notice, sold up, decided to try and write the book you've been meaning to write and opted for the quiet life. Is that it?'

'More or less.' His smile was uncertain and she realized she might have sounded condescending, rude even. It was David's influence, of course, for he had no time for so called opters-out. It was not something he considered an option for people in their prime. In fact, Francesca did wonder about his *retiring* and whether or not he would have been quickly bored out of his mind. 'I thought long and hard about it,' Gareth went on, cheeks flushed. 'There were other things happening in my life at the time so it wasn't a spur of the moment thing.'

'You haven't regretted it?'

'Absolutely not.'

She noted the glance towards her left hand. Yes, she had signed in as Mrs Porter and she was wearing her wedding band and the unusual antique diamond engagement ring that had belonged to David's late mother. It was a privilege to wear it and she had felt enormously touched when David produced it.

'I admire your guts,' she told Gareth, taking heed of his defensive tone and back-tracking. 'It can't have been an easy decision. I've worked for years in the city too and I know how it gets to you.'

Blessedly the phone rang at that moment and with a muttered excuse-me he was off. Francesca poured herself another cup of tea from the pretty china pot alarmed to find her hands shaking. What on earth was she doing here? Suddenly she was a small girl again sitting here in this room watching television or reading a book and her mother was there or, years earlier before James, her father. Curtains drawn across on a winter's evening hearing the wind howling from the moor, night sounds that had scared her when she was little. In summer, the windows would be thrown open and the balmy air, fresh and sweet, would rush in.

Without warning, faintness came over her and she had to take a few deep breaths as panic battered her from all directions and she felt as if she was spinning like water going down a drain. She lowered her head, closed her eyes.

This was a mistake.

There were smothered voices here, echoes of the past and unseen eyes watching. She remembered her parents and wished their marriage had been happier. As a child she could not help and later she had compounded her mother's unhappiness when she had allowed the accident to happen to James. As a direct result of that, her mother had shrunk before her eyes, all that wonderful exuberance stripped away.

She lifted her head as the spinning mercifully ceased, her heart stopped its alarmed hammering and she could breathe more easily. Out in the hall, she could hear Gareth's voice on the telephone and she roused herself, dug in her handbag and quickly checked her hair, her lipstick, although she could do nothing about the shocked look in her eyes.

The room had been neutralized, stripped of its heart. There were not many original features left and yet the alcoves were still there, although the shelves that had once been crowded with family paraphernalia were long gone.

Underneath all the changes, it was still Francesca's home.

What was she hoping to achieve by coming back?

Whichever way you looked at it, it was a big mistake.

Chapter Eight

ROSEMARY WETHERALL TURNED out to be a very chatty, energetic heavy-set lady in her mid-fifties. Greying hair cut in an uncompromising chin-length bob framed an interesting intelligent face. Her arrival did not go unnoticed, gales of laughter and her strident voice coming close to raising the roof. Taking a breather after her long day in what was the guests' sitting room, Francesca listened in with a smile as Gareth took the lady's particulars before leading her upstairs to the Bluebell room.

She collared Francesca in that sitting room about five o'clock that evening coming to sit opposite on one of the comfortable sofas. According to Gareth, the Sandersons occupied just a couple of rooms at the back of the house when the B&B was occupied giving the guests sole use of the sitting and dining-rooms.

Francesca put down the magazine she had been reading although reading was the wrong word for she had just been leafing through and scarcely seeing it, her mind elsewhere. She was tired from the drive and the excitement, but as the B&B was just that, bed and breakfast, she would have to go out later to eat.

'Hello there, I'm exhausted,' the newly arrived lady came bounding in, sinking thankfully into a chair tossing aside the mountain of cushions. 'I've ordered coffee and cake. Gareth asked if you wanted some too.'

'No thanks. I'm fine.'

'Don't mind me. Carry on reading by all means.'

'I've finished. Have you had a long journey?'

The polite enquiry was the signal the lady needed. Within moments, even before the coffee arrived, Francesca had ascertained that she was a professor, a lecturer in politics and economics at a northern university taking time out to do some walking in an area of the country that she knew very little about.

'It was an awful drive down,' she told Francesca. 'It went on *forever*. But it looks as if it will be worth it. I find myself enchanted already. We're in for a good dry spell apparently. Are you staying long, Mrs Porter?'

'I'm not sure how long exactly,' Francesca said carefully, smiling but mindful that Miss Wetherall, a nice enough woman, was probably not averse to having a walking companion and she had no intention of being roped into that. 'Are you?'

'Just a couple of nights.,' she explained. 'I've got two walks planned and then I'm moving on to base myself near the Lizard to do some of the Cornish coastal walk.'

'Are you meeting up with anyone?'

'Absolutely not. I like to do my own thing. I usually walk with other people which is fine but it does have disadvantages. It means that you can't always go at your own pace. I like to stop and admire the view.'

'Isn't it a bit risky walking on your own?'

'Not a bit of it.' She seemed surprised. 'People are neurotic these days about the dangers we women face when we go it alone. Statistically you know there are no more murders nowadays than there were fifty years ago and no more child abductions either. I reckon I will be much safer here than in any city you care to mention. In any case, if anybody cares to attack me I shall give them a run for their money I can tell you.'

Francesca smiled. She imagined she would.

'Obviously I am not completely foolish,' Rosemary went on with a wry smile. 'I shall let Gareth know tomorrow what my intended route is and what time I expect to be back. I know it's supposed to be a lovely day but it's wise to have a back-up in case I fall and break my leg and find myself stranded in the middle of nowhere.'

'Have you a mobile?'

'Oh yes but from past experience reception can be a problem when you need it most.'

'Don't I know it?'

'I'm Rosemary,' the lady said with a smile.

'Francesca.' For a moment she was tempted to tell Rosemary about yesterday and the eventual phone call to the distraught Selina, but Rosemary did not give her the chance, ploughing on and asking her if she did any walking.

'I haven't walked seriously for years. I used to do some long walks with a group when I was at university up in Scotland but I was a lot younger then.'

Rosemary laughed. 'You are a mere babe. Do you fancy a walk? You could join me if you like? It's only about ten miles, not very strenuous.'

'No thanks. I don't have any suitable shoes,' Francesca said knowing it was a lame excuse, but sensing that the offer was made out of politeness rather than a genuine need for companionship. 'Sorry but I really don't have the time for walking. I have things to do.'

'Fair enough. As I say I'm quite happy walking on my own. However ...' she flashed a rueful glance Francesca's way.

'Eating out alone is another matter entirely. Would you care to join me this evening at one of the restaurants in town that Gareth has recommended?'

It was all said in a friendly fashion, no strings attached, and Francesca felt a little guilty at putting her off but just now it was the last thing she wanted as she felt she was in danger of confessing all to an amiable stranger and Rosemary did have a dangerously sympathetic air about her.

'I'm so sorry, I would love to but I have plans,' she told her, smiling yet uncomfortable in having to keep refusing the poor woman her company. 'I used to live round here and I'm meeting an old friend.'

'How lovely. It's always super to catch up with old friends.'

Francesca was not sure whether or not she believed her, but it was the best she could manage. The lie, though, as lies do, created a difficulty and she was forced to go out of town later to avoid an accidental meeting with Rosemary, ending up eating a fish and chip supper in the car. It was astonishing that the fish and chip shop she remembered was still there in a nearby village, but she felt out of place now in the little queue, gone so long from here that she was instantly picked out as a visitor.

The chip shop was family owned and, to her surprise, she recognized the man behind the counter, older but unmistakably the same man who had sold her and Izzy fish and chips twenty two years before.

'Hello,' she said brightly when it was her turn.

'What can I get you, madam?' he asked with an answering smile.

Clearly, he did not recognize *her*.

No matter for, sitting eating them back in the car, the chips hot, salty and vinegary, the fish white and flaky in its crisp batter it was one of the best meals she had had for some time.

Returning to Lilac House, hearing the voices of the other guests in the sitting-room where it seemed the professor was holding court she crept past and up to her room, quickly using the bathroom she was sharing with Rosemary before locking herself in her room.

She was worried now that she had been unnecessarily abrupt and had somehow upset the lady but it was not fair to spoil her walking holiday and having to listen – however sympathetically – to someone else's problems would certainly do that.

Unburdening herself to a stranger though was tempting for, for whatever reason, she had been unable to talk about things that really mattered to the people she loved. The die was cast as soon as it happened. There had been one moment when it might have been different when her mother had asked if she wanted to talk, if she had anything to say, but the opportunity passed and after that it became harder and harder as her mother became more and more detached from her. She went through the motions, never neglecting her physically, keeping her clothed and fed but emotionally the neglect was complete.

Francesca had not talked, really talked, to anybody about James and the effect his accident had on her. The nearest she came to it was in the years she spent with her first love Andrew but in the event she was too ashamed of how she had acted, worried that he might see her differently. For wasn't it true that she alone had been responsible for shattering her mother's hopes and dreams for her only son and destroying her mother's love for her? Not only that, she had single-handedly been responsible for snuffing out all her mother's exuberance.

Her mother, a bright light of a lady, was never the same afterwards; she became a mere shadow, and it was all her fault.

Not many daughters could lay claim to that.

It had been far too great a burden to bear for the young girl she had been at the time and she had never truly come to terms with it. Counselling had been offered, but her mother had refused outside help. They just had to get on with life for nothing could change what had happened.

If only....

It was a long time before she slept.

Chapter Nine

NEXT MORNING BY the time she got herself down to the dining-room the other guests were already out and about. The guests, as Gareth had explained last night, generally liked to breakfast together sitting at the big rectangular table and the Sandersons approved of that because everybody got to know everybody else. If it was a wet day, breakfast could stretch well into the morning. As well as Rosemary there were two older couples so that the four available rooms were all occupied.

It was just as well that, with high pressure anchored over them, the next few days promised to be warm and sunny and everyone was anxious to make early starts. After her tearful outburst yesterday, coming out of nowhere as it had, Francesca was nervous that she might lose it suddenly in a room full of strangers and make a fool of herself. Tears embarrassed everybody and she had no wish to let people know her situation.

'Sorry I'm late,' she said, checking the empty dining-room as Gareth appeared, looking as if he had been up for hours wearing a blue and white striped apron and a welcoming smile.

'No problem. Can I get you a full English breakfast?'

'Goodness no. Please don't bother cooking just for me. Toast will do. And some coffee would be lovely.'

'Coming up. Did you sleep well?'

'Yes thank you.' Another quick lie, but a white one for there was no need to explain her sleep patterns to him. Ever since David's death it took her forever to get off and, irritatingly, she usually woke up early too. She often dreamed of David and last night had been no exception, although there had been no repetition of that night just a couple of days following his death when, turning in a trance-like state in the early hours, she had felt David's presence strongly beside her – his hand had been in hers and surely she had not imagined the weight of his body on his side of the bed. A visitation of his spiritual being maybe, although she had not discussed it with anybody particularly Selina who would think it creepy and, in any case, it felt too private a thing. She remembered waking up the following morning relaxed and with a smile on her face.

'Just toast it is,' Gareth repeated, looking closely at her. 'If you are quite sure?'

'Quite sure, thank you.'

She took stock of the dining room when he was gone, but it was all different, the solid old-fashioned furniture mixing surprisingly easily with the modern décor and again there was a big display of flowers on the wide window ledge. She asked about the flowers wondering whether he was into that as well, but he explained that a woman from the florists came and changed the displays every week. Pamela liked those little important touches.

After presenting her with toast, thickly cut granary bread with a little pot of marmalade, Gareth, asking her permission first, hovered. So, as she munched on her toast, finding herself hungrier than she had thought, he quietly went about his business, clearing away dishes and tidying up, having provided not only the toast and coffee but a newspaper. It was not her usual but it gave her something to do, a distraction from having to make conversation. This was the only time of day she occasionally missed cigarettes, but it was a fleeting fancy and she knew she would never go back to them.

'So, you're from London, Mrs Porter?' he said at length, giving in and sitting himself on one of the dining chairs opposite, probably realizing that she was in no particular hurry to go anywhere.

'I'm not from London, but I've been working there for many years,' she told him and then, as the silence lengthened, she felt obliged to carry on, hiding the slightest sigh as she put the newspaper aside. 'I'm in the process of selling my husband's house there. I'm being pushed on a completion date so I have to get my finger out and get something else before I find myself out on the street. Hardly that,' she added with a little smile. 'But I am beginning to feel a little pressured.'

'Moving house is a horror. They say it rates only second to losing a spouse,' he said with a shudder.

'Yes, well ...' she felt herself flushing.

'Are you looking for something down here?'

'Good heavens, no. We ...' she hesitated but it was stupid not to say it and she imagined she could rely on his discretion. 'My husband died recently. We had the house up for sale because we were intending to move to Yorkshire. We had it all arranged, had got the house up there, but that was really David's dream. I don't think it's mine and I couldn't face moving up there on my own.'

'I'm sorry to hear that. I didn't mean to upset you.'

'It's all right. You haven't.' She flashed him a smile.

'It must be hard,' he said quietly. 'Your husband can't have been very old.'

'He was older than me,' she said and there was no need to say any more than that. 'I think I need time out as they say. I feel as if the rug's been whipped from under my feet, but my plan is to go back to London and maybe even rent for a while until I decide what to do next. I don't want to go rushing into things and then regret it.'

'No, but don't hang about too long. Go with your instincts. This place is up for sale if you're interested in running a B&B.'

'Is it?' she asked sharply. 'There's no sign.'

'No but it's on the agency's books. The Sandersons didn't want a sign outside because it puts people off booking in. They're just coming back after the cruise to sort things out and then they are off to live in France.'

'Thanks for breakfast, Gareth.' She handed him the paper and pushed back her chair. 'I'm off out then. See you later.'

'There are some leaflets on the hall table,' he said. 'It's a glorious day. I would suggest you take a trip out to the coast and make the most of it.'

'I might.' She smiled at him, aware of the approving glance. The sudden appearance of the sun had sent everybody off into a premature summer mood and Francesca was glad that, although her excursion had been taken on impulse and she had not actually packed a bag of holiday clothes, she had some linen trousers with her and a striped loose cover-up, and a selection of silver bracelets jingling on her wrist. She seemed to have inherited her mother's haphazard attitude to jewellery, but today her whole outfit felt totally wrong, too bright, too garish, too much fun and she understood why widowed ladies used to retreat into black. She felt she ought to be drenched in it, but David would not have wanted her to do that. One of the things she must do today was to buy some more clothes to tide her over the next few days.

Looking out at the bright morning sunshine, she fiddled around in her bag for the sunglasses she usually carried round to help with winter driving.

'Bye then Mrs Porter. Have a nice day.'

'Thank you. See you later.'

She supposed he might wonder why she was not heading for her car round the back but she had something to do down in town before she set off.

Go with your instincts, he had said.

So, first of all, she had to pay a visit to the estate agent's.

Back at the house Francesca met up with Gareth just after lunch when he had completed his chores – he seemed to be a very efficient one-man band – and was relaxing in what was now called the sun-room, the old lean-to which had been very prettily renovated. Mrs Sanderson had gone rather over the top here with floral excess and Gareth, feet up, was doing a crossword.

The sun-room was not for guests being in what was officially designated the Sandersons' portion of the house and, although Francesca caught sight of Gareth as she passed through the hall she felt she ought not to intrude on his private time, he must have seen or heard her, though, for he called out and waved her in.

'Come in. Hi there …' he looked up and smiled and she motioned him to stay as he threatened to get up. Somehow, it pleased her, the little gentlemanly gesture, the sort of thing David would do.

'This is lovely.'

Francesca crossed to the French doors glancing out at the garden with a critical eye. On closer inspection, it was racing away and needed a good tidy. She knew nothing about gardening, had never had a garden of her own, but like a lot of people who watch television gardening programmes she felt an urge to pull up a few weeds and see what plants were actually hidden there.

'There is a man who comes in a couple of times a week,' Gareth said, perhaps sensing critical vibes escaping her. 'His wife's been ill so he's got a bit behind.'

'Yes, you did tell me.'

'I'm just about keeping the front in order, but if he doesn't turn up this week, I'm going to have to do something with that lot. Pamela would have a fit if she saw it just now. Are you a gardener?'

'An armchair one,' she said, sitting down and wasting no time in acquainting him with what she had been up to that morning. She needed to tell somebody before she exploded with the news.

'Good grief, I was only joking when I said you should buy it,' he said, looking at her with both amazement and consternation. He was wearing pale blue jeans today, the lived in variety, the old sandals and a clean white tee shirt that showed off his nicely toned body and he looked good. So good in fact that she chose not to look directly at him worried that she might give something away. If a woman always knew when a man admired her then surely the opposite would apply. It was disconcerting to say the least. 'But I thought you said you weren't interested in living down here? What made you change your mind?'

'I know I said that, but I didn't know what I wanted until it stared me in the face. There's more to it, you see.'

'I thought there might be.' He hesitated, probably sensing her reluctance. 'Do you want to tell me?'

'I know this house, Gareth. It was my childhood home.'

'Ah. Now I understand.' His smile broadened. 'I thought you seemed very familiar with it for someone who'd never seen it before.'

She laughed and suddenly the words spilled out. 'I was just

passing and couldn't resist stopping by to see it again and when I saw it was a B&B I just had to stay in it once more. Then when you said it was up for sale, well ...' she waved a hand around. 'I was born up in the room you call the Bluebell room. Honestly, whose idea was it to give the rooms names like that?'

'Pamela's. As you can see she loves flowers and, after all, she named it Lilac House so she's just continuing the theme.'

'It's always been called Lilac House.'

'You're serious about buying it then?'

'Absolutely. The agent's going to get in touch with the Sandersons as soon as he can although they have asked not to be contacted just now. As you know, they are on the high seas somewhere and they can be contacted in an emergency but this hardly counts as that. It can wait a few days and as I am offering to pay the full asking price there should be no problem.' She smiled a little as she saw him raise his eyebrows. 'I know. I should have haggled. It's been on the market for a while so I could probably have negotiated a reduced price but I didn't want to hang about and risk losing it.'

'You've really taken me by surprise. I don't know what to say. Are you going to carry on running it as a B&B?'

'No, absolutely not.' She had not considered that at all. 'It's my home, Gareth. And, do you know, it still felt like my home the minute I walked through the door. I can't wait to hear from the Sandersons when they dock.'

'They'll be thrilled, but just a word of caution. I know you said you've sold your place but it's not over until you've got the signatures on the contract. Sorry, I don't want to sound pessimistic, I wouldn't like you to get your hopes up though, and then for it all to go wrong.'

'It shouldn't,' she assured him confidently. 'In any case, I can complete whether or not I sell the house.'

'Oh, that's good.' He looked as if he might query that and for a moment Francesca regretted saying it for it implied she might have more money than sense. 'I wish you well with it.'

'I'd rather you didn't mention it to the other guests. I shall have to come up with far too many explanations. And please don't tell anybody about my husband.'

'Of course not. I shan't breathe a word. It will take a while, but once things get moving, do give me a shout if you need any help.'

'Thank you. I probably will now that I'm on my own.'

Her bravado instantly deflated as she realized what that meant and she felt again the ache that had preceded her bout of tears.

'Are you all right, Mrs Porter?' he said, watching her closely and for two pins she would have said no she wasn't all right and let him take her in his arms if only to give her a much needed hug.

'I'm fine. And do please call me Francesca. Especially if we're to be neighbours.'

'Hardly neighbours,' he corrected her with a smile. 'We are in different counties for a start. It takes roughly an hour to get to my place. Once you get off the main road it's all little lanes and the last bit is down a dirt track full of potholes.'

An hour seemed nothing and she had the feeling that they might become friends given time. Anything else would have to wait. For goodness sake, David's ashes would still be catching the wind and floating on air on Ilkley Moor.

'Good luck with it, Francesca. And don't look so worried. I'm sure everything will be fine.'

That made a change. Everybody else would think her completely bonkers.

*

Refusing Gareth's offer to make her a pot of tea, she insisted he stay put and she went up to her room soon afterwards to contemplate exactly what she had done. She was unable to resist giving a little skip of delight when she reached the upper landing and stole a glance out of the window.

This would be hers very soon.

She would keep the room which had been allotted to her as it was because she liked the poppy wallpaper and felt it would make a lovely little retreat. It was madness to have a house as large as this when she was on her own, but she did not care what other people might think. Selina, once she got over it, would love it. It would be her idea of bliss, the sort of country cottage she had long desired, the second home that she had been urging a more cautious Clive to buy for years.

She must invite the whole family over as soon as she had things settled.

She stared at herself in the mirror giving a rueful smile. Her eyes, she noted, still had that immensely sad look, brightness temporarily snuffed out, but her hair was recovering and looking a good deal better. She had worn a hat at the funeral which, with her hair tucked under its brim, hid a multitude of sins. She wore it for two reasons; one to hide her hair for having a bad hair day at your husband's funeral is really rubbing it in. The second reason for the hat was because she felt that David's friends would approve of that and she really did not want them to think badly of her. There were a few whispered mentions of a memorial service at a later date, but she could not bring herself to discuss it and had quietly dropped the idea. Appearing centre stage at the funeral was bad enough without having to go through it all again.

Francesca had been insistent though that she was not going to take anything to help her over it as several of her friends suggested. There was no point in dulling the pain because eventually she knew she would have to face up to it fair and square. She needed to experience, almost in a masochistic way, the jagged edge of grief, that first overwhelming emotion. It was like wading through a gigantic wave that almost knocks you off your feet, but you have no choice but to fight your way through it to reach the shallows and some sort of peace. She used that powerful image daily and although it was early days and she was still buffeted by the wave she knew she would get there eventually.

Chapter Ten

BACK IN LONDON, the house felt strange without him, stuffy, too, for it had been closed up for a while. She noticed there was also now an echo as most of the furniture had been removed, leaving just a few essentials. His cleaner had been in and the place was spotless.

It was a beautiful house in many ways, graciously proportioned, and yet she had never felt completely at home in it, an intruder in David's bachelor lifestyle. Francesca went round it, room by room, opening up windows and letting the city air sweep greedily in – air which felt surprisingly clean and sweet – before having a lie down fully clothed allowing herself a quiet unrestrained weep. Her mother was wrong about locking your feelings away. She was beginning to realize that crying acted like a release valve. It helped and afterwards she got up and made herself a cup of coffee in David's underused kitchen.

She felt a bit better.

She had stuffed all the condolence cards – from David's colleagues and institutions mainly, very few personal ones – in a drawer beside the congratulations cards they had received at their wedding and she now retrieved them to take with her. She doubted she would be in a fit state to read them for some time to come, but she did not wish to dispose of them.

It was tough for other people, too, his funeral following so close on the wedding and her female colleagues at work found it difficult to cope with. Once they had got over the surprise of her marrying an older man, they had all become terribly positive, rallied round, clubbed together and bought them bed-linen from The White Company. They were not at the wedding because it was such a quiet affair but, even though she had resigned and was no longer at the office they came along to support her at the funeral, unsure what to wear and playing safe with black, purple or grey, hatless, unused to funerals and uncharacteristically quiet as a result.

A few days later, as promised, they came round to see her at home, at David's house, phoning first and asking anxiously if they might just pop in. They trooped in and arranged themselves on David's sofas, different women somehow out of the office and she did not know them in a social sense for she had rarely joined in their get-togethers out of work. Francesca had never quite got over feeling uneasy in company. She wasn't an Izzy, the sort of girl who could fit in anywhere, the sort of girl who would have a little group gathering round her within minutes. Francesca was always the one standing at the edge of things, often alone, holding a glass at social functions and smiling. Her father was just the same, happy to remain in the vivacious shadow of her mother. She had never found her shyness a problem in business though, and it was as if her calmer quieter approach appealed to clients more than the brash go-for-it attitude of some of her colleagues.

Her former colleagues were uneasy because, all younger than her, not one of them was a wife yet let alone a widow. They admired the house, the furniture, the Chinese rugs, the grandeur of it all. They maybe admired it too much and

Francesca quickly explained that none of this was her choice and that it was all a little fussy for her taste. Then, as she saw the relief on their faces, she felt guilty for criticizing David's taste for he had loved his home and every piece of furniture was precious to him.

An awkward silence then threatened and it was left to Francesca to try to put them at their ease, making coffee and handing round chocolate biscuits which was a bit naughty of her because they were all on some diet or another.

'Oh, what the hell,' one of them gave in with a grimace and the others, given the go-ahead, followed suit for it was something to do, something to keep them from the awful job of finding something to say.

With the disgracefully rapid disappearance of the biscuits, somebody then had the temerity to laugh which made the others frown and shush her as if Francesca could not cope with laughter.

Why did everybody think that?

'I wish you'd met David, girls,' she told them cheerfully, letting it be known that they could mention his name without her falling apart. 'He was such a charming man.'

'At least he's left you with all this,' one of them said unaware of the warning glances from the others. 'He obviously wasn't short of money. I know it's only a small consolation, but it's better than being broke, isn't it? Well, it is,' she added defiantly at the shocked expressions. 'I'm only trying to help.'

'Thanks,' Francesca told her gratefully. 'And you're right. At least I don't have any money worries.'

At last, she could stand it no longer, she understood their awkwardness and knowing they were desperate to leave she didn't mind that in the future they would give her a wide berth. They seemed relieved to hear that she would not be coming back to work and, at the door they each gave her a hug and promised to keep in touch.

A promise none of them would keep.

Duty done.

She smiled and waved as they piled into their cars, guessing that they were all breathing huge sighs of relief. She knew she would not see any of them again, but then such was the fleeting nature of some friendships.

Others lasted forever.

She and Izzy for instance. What had happened on that day had bound them together and even if the links had loosened with the years they were still there.

Sometimes she wanted to resurrect the relationship, take it back to those happy childhood years, but she knew that was impossible.

They were grown ups now. She was a widow and Izzy a mum of four.

They could never go back.

Fortunately, David's personal files were well organized as Francesca would have expected them to be and up-to-the-minute at that which meant the sorting out was accomplished with the minimum of fuss as she posted copies of the death certificate off to all interested parties. Even with Selina's professional help though, it still took considerable time and effort and there were a few hitches, but perhaps that was a good thing because being so busy meant that she didn't have time to sit and think. On top of all the usual stuff associated with a death, there was also the sale of this house to complete, complicated by his demise, and the disposal of most of the furniture to arrange although the new people had happily agreed to take on some of the fixtures and fittings.

She had been working up to persuading him to have a major throw-out prior to the move north so, although she mouthed a silent sorry to him, she was not in fact sorry to see most of it go. It raised a healthy sum at auction, but she did keep his beloved desk that she could not bear to part with and, perhaps unwisely, the bed they had shared.

Furniture was one thing, but his clothes and shoes were another and she didn't know where to start on that. Seeing how it was upsetting her, Selina in her brisk business-like mode got her husband Clive to deal with it. She took Francesca out for the day.

'A bit of retail therapy will do you a world of good, darling,' she said.

Francesca had been irritated at that, as if something as lightweight as shopping could help, but in an odd way it had. Egged on by the expert, she bought several new outfits, enjoyed a girly lunch at one of Selina's favourite restaurants, got ever so slightly sozzled and when they returned, heavily laden, Clive had worked his magic. The wardrobes and drawers in David's dressing-room were empty, all the masculine stuff, razors, aftershaves and so on removed from the bathroom. Even so, Clive had missed one or two little things, his spare glasses in their case for instance and boxes of cufflinks which he kept in a small easily missed drawer in his dressing room.

A new start was what she needed and she began to feel excited at the prospect of moving to Lilac House and putting her own stamp on it. She bought a heap of glossy magazines seeking out some ideas for furnishing it. She could easily afford to employ an interior designer to help – Selina of course knew of this marvellous woman – but she had all the time in the world and she wanted to do it herself. After the bustle and floral chaos that was Pamela Sanderson the house needed calming down a little but she hated minimalism and would have to get the balance just right.

With most of the furniture gone, she moved out of the bedroom she had shared with David and, wrapped in a quilt, camped instead in one of the guest rooms where his presence was not so keenly felt.

The new people planned to turn this room into a nursery so she imagined it would soon be stripped of its present wallpaper and replaced with a pretty baby theme in pink or blue. Quickly she whipped through similar nursery schemes in her magazines for she would not need them.

With lamps lit and a cup of cocoa at her side, she spread the magazines on the floor, scissors at the ready to cut out pictures of her favourite schemes, and, because her sleep pattern was still wildly astray, she was still sitting there in the small hours planning what she would do.

Most of the necessary business to do with the house and David's effects was concluded within days and Francesca was anxious to get back to Devon – home – but first she needed to fit in a visit to Selina's. That was no mean task with Selina so busy working and Francesca's offer of having lunch together somewhere special met with a muted response. With one day only remaining before Francesca was leaving she was beginning to think that they would not be able to fit in a face-to-face chat with not even a hint of a window in Selina's diary until her phone call that morning.

'Darling, I've had this shocking cold so I've been ordered to take the day off,' Selina had said. 'Do come round if you don't mind catching it.'

In fact, Selina was over the worst of it and feeling considerably better by the time Francesca arrived, but she had distributed her germs far and wide over the previous couple of days and they were all becoming extremely annoyed at her continued presence in the office.

They sat in Selina's kitchen drinking coffee, not just your average coffee either because Selina took her coffee making seriously. The cups were unusual, bought at a French market, a bargain for which she had haggled. They were cream, as big as soup dishes and the generous cup would provide Francesca with her caffeine intake for the whole day. She reckoned that, as she was doing cold turkey with no helpful calming pills following David's death that she was surely entitled to her daily shot of caffeine.

'Have a biscuit,' Selina said, pushing the container her way. Only women like Selina could manage to look chic with a red nose and little make-up but somehow she did. She was dressed in a leisure outfit, pyjamas for want of a better word although expensive Italian ballerina pumps graced her feet rather than slippers.

'Thanks.'

Selina's kitchen was the hub of the house and as she listened to her friend, Francesca found herself thinking back to the dinner parties she had attended here with David when even he had to shrug off his prejudices and eat here in the kitchen. They were jolly noisy affairs with eight people crowded round the big table sitting on roughly matching chairs. The food was plentiful and Selina called it rustic in a throwaway manner as if she had just clobbered it together with one hand tied behind her back when even the bread rolls were home-made.

Francesca felt more at home amongst those people, the lower end of David's social acquaintances, and had been more genuinely welcomed into this group. She had started to relax knowing that eventually entertaining like this would become part of her life and, for all their sakes, she would learn to do it properly. The kitchen in the house up in Yorkshire, the one they very nearly bought, had had a huge kitchen with potential for a large table and she had thought that perhaps she might wean David away from the formality of the dining-room someday.

That had been a forlorn hope.

Selina's kitchen was the size of Francesca's previous flat with a cheerfully messy area off to one side which she called the snug. It was where she could keep an eye on the children whilst she cooked. It was full of battered sofas, cushions and colouring books, building blocks and heaps of board games with the contents spilling out. Somewhere amongst the mountain of soft toys a cat, a real one, or two, might lurk.

Clive did something in the city very boring, but very lucrative, but he looked harassed all the time and Selina told her that David suddenly popping off without warning had scared the shit out of him. He had stopped the jogging which he was only half hearted about anyway but was starting to cycle to the office where he had taken to using the stairs instead of the lift.

'Silly man,' Selina said with a fond wifely smile. 'The office is on the third floor. He's knackered before he starts.'

Clive was driving her mad, she confessed. The house was now a cholesterol-free, Flora-rich zone and he had bought a blood pressure measuring device and he took his BP every morning, sometimes several times if he didn't get a sensible reading straight off. He was even muttering about a personal fitness trainer because he couldn't fit the gym into his schedule.

'Will you have a word with him, Francesca?'

'About what? He won't take any notice of me.'

'He might or at least he's far too polite to tell you where to stick your advice. The poor darling has to get a grip,' Selina said. 'We're all on death row if you like and, like most of those poor souls we don't know how long we've got either. The appeals system in some of those American states can go on for years and years.'

'Don't get technical. Those poor souls you talk about have committed murder,' Francesca reminded her.

'They are *alleged* to have committed murder. You have to question some of those verdicts.'

Francesca shook her head as, undeterred, Selina in full grumble-mode happily moved on to the horrific problems facing them regarding their boys' education. Smiling sympathetically but hardly listening, Francesca switched off and looked round the kitchen. The whole kitchen, the units, the bespoke shelving, granite work surfaces, limestone floor and top of the range appliances cost a bomb but they did not actually look pristine for Selina had a carefree attitude to cleaning. A few germs, she maintained, did nobody any harm and we were far too anxious these days.

She practised what she preached. The cleaner's work from the previous day was sabotaged already with barely an inch available on the worktops, children's junk all over the place, crayons dipped in the sugar bowl, a collection of homemade items – unrecognizable as to what – and scribbled paintings stuck on a pin-board. On the floor, as Selina continued her rant, one of the cats was upturned, licking its nether regions with great delicacy. The children were out with the nanny so they had a bit of peace.

'Are you listening?'

Francesca sat up straighter. 'Of course.'

'So, Francesca, I'm not going to say you're barking mad

moving back there. You must do what you think fit,' Selina said turning her cold-induced irritation towards Francesca.

'Which means you do think I'm barking mad?'

'Not exactly, but in my opinion you should have taken more time to think about it. It was an impulse buy and what you should have done was buy yourself a huge box of chocolates instead of a house. You are grieving, darling, in shock, and you have to be careful you don't make a cock-up of a decision. Whenever I've bought something on impulse it's always turned out to be a complete disaster. Remember that flowery frock? Six hundred quid and I look like Bo Peep in it.'

'Do you mean that pink one? I think it's lovely.'

'I only bought it because I was in mourning because one of the guinea pigs had died that very morning. So let that be a lesson to you. I can see you don't believe me,' she said with a slight smile. 'I'll find you the picture in the nursery rhyme book. My dress is a dead ringer and it took Cosmo to tell me as much. Anyway ...' she frowned. 'Country living is not all it's cracked up to be.'

'You've changed your tune,' Francesca reminded her. 'You're always on at Clive to buy something in the country.'

'I know but seriously it would just cause more problems. Imagine the hassle of getting the children ready to go every weekend. It would be torture. This vision I have of sunny meadows, buttercups and lazy picnics is totally barmy. The reality is different. For one thing, all those farm animals give me the creeps. Have you ever seen a cow close up? And I don't mean Angela Dickson, darling.'

Francesca smiled a little.

'I know your own flat is sold but there's nothing to stop you from buying another one round here,' Selina persisted. 'Why don't you? You can afford something nicer and you would have me close at hand. I can help you look if you like. You've not signed on the dotted line yet so it's not too late to back out of this silly Devon thing. You can plead temporary insanity. Everybody will forgive you under the circumstances. If you like I'll explain for you. You can leave the whole thing to me.'

'No, Selina. I'm not going to back out now. I've met the Sandersons and they are very nice people.'

'It's business, darling. Nothing to do with now nice people are.' Defeated, Selina sighed and settled into a sulk, looking suddenly very like Crispin. 'I'll have you know it's not going to be easy for me to get over to Devon with my tribe. It's such an almighty trek. Frankly it's easier to cross the Atlantic.'

'It was a chance in a lifetime and I had to move fast because I didn't want to miss it. Look, I don't know if I'm doing the right thing either and I don't want to start having second thoughts. Please try to understand and be happy for me.'

'Sorry. I didn't mean to put you off. How are you these days?'

Francesca shook her head knowing that, as Selina had not experienced close family bereavement – for you could hardly include the death of a guinea pig in that – it would be impossible to explain how she felt. It was early days as everybody kept saying and she knew that the hurt and pain would become a little less sharp as time went by but that, for a very long time, the grief could come at you like a tsunami and for a while it would be as bad as it ever was.

'I'm still as annoyed as hell,' she told Selina. 'Why David? He was fit for his age. He looked after himself, didn't drink or smoke excessively and we should have had years together.'

'And that's what you looked forward to?' Selina opened the container and foraged for a biscuit. 'He would have been eighty when you were sixty.'

'So? I knew that when I married him.'

'I have to say this, Francesca, because it looks as if you've shut your mind to it, but David Porter was an exceptionally difficult man. Let me tell you he was impossible to work with, never mind all that 'wasn't he wonderful' business at the funeral. He was so bloody irritatingly good at his job, but he had a particular way of doing it and he made a lot of enemies and there were a lot of people glad to see the back of him. In other words, professionally, he was a total shit.'

'For goodness sake, Selina ...'

'Sorry, I must do something about my language before the children start picking up on it. What I'm trying to say is that he would have made your life a misery long term. I did try to warn you. Take all that ghastly furniture for one. He would never have let you get rid of that. You would have been stuck with it.' She stirred her coffee thoughtfully. 'What's happening with those paintings? I hope you've put them somewhere safe. They're worth a lot, you know.'

'I do know. It's all in hand. They're going under the hammer next week.'

Selina gave what might have been construed as a snort of disapproval causing Francesca to glance sharply at her.

'Have you a problem with that?'

'None at all. They are yours now so it's your business, Francesca.'

Exactly.

'He should never have got married,' Selina continued, a faraway look on her face. She was out of sorts today and coping with her in a melancholy mood was not helping Francesca's cause one little bit.

'Oh come on, Selina, he was desperate to get married. And he didn't exactly force me at gunpoint either.'

'He once asked me, you know. He got down on his knees, the whole caboodle.'

'I didn't know that. Obviously you said no.'

She smiled. 'Ah, well … I asked for time to think about it and then the next day he came up to me in court and whispered that I was perfectly right, it was an insane idea and would I ever forgive him. So, he sort of withdrew the question before I had time to answer it. He must have been thinking it over and realized what a mistake he'd made. He was a devious bugger.'

'Would you have said yes?'

'I don't know. There wasn't much happening in my life at the time so I suppose I might have. He was charming, wasn't he? And so powerful and that is a real turn on for me. That's why I married Clive in the end. There's something very attractive about a man who can command a six figure salary.'

They laughed, the sombre mood broken, although Francesca was still stung by what Selina had said; sometimes her directness was hard to take.

'I asked for time to think about it too,' she said. 'But he kept on at me and of course eventually I said yes.'

'Poor David.' Selina's eyes filled with tears and she reached for a tissue, blew her nose. 'Have you had a good cry yet?'

Francesca nodded, unwilling to admit it.

'Thank the Lord for that. I told you to let it out. Did you feel better for it?'

'I don't know. I suppose so. I'd only got used to being with him and now I've got to get used to being without him.'

'They say it gets easier,' she said, face flushing. 'Oh God, I swore I would never say that to you. But they do say that, don't they, whoever they are.'

'People who have gone through it presumably,' Francesca

said, remembering how grief had affected her mother, how she had drowned in it, how it had changed her, hardened her heart and all because she was unable to forgive. 'Come and stay with me when I get settled in Devon,' she went on, trying to find a lifeline for Selina. 'You can help me choose some colour schemes. You know how I worry about that.'

'I would love to, darling,' she said and Francesca could tell she was working up to saying no. 'But I have the children and arrangements are so complicated. Once my plans are made ...' she indicated a huge spread-sheet pinned on the board. 'They're written in stone. We're spending a chunk of the summer holidays in Italy at Clive's mother's villa so that's my holiday entitlement gone in one fell swoop. Thank God we don't have to fit round school holidays yet but that will come soon enough. Then when we get back there'll be a million and one things to sort out so as you see, fitting in a visit to Devon, dragging us over there, is just impossible.'

'That's OK.' Francesca smiled, hiding her disappointment. She wanted Selina to see the house, to be enchanted by it so that perhaps she might understand. The chat had proved to be disturbing rather than consoling. She thought Selina was wrong about David. Given time, she might have been able to change him.

Selina's negative reaction also prompted a reappraisal of the move. When she needed to talk whom did she immediately think of? Selina, of course because she was near at hand and, providing she had a slot in her schedule, was always willing to talk; she was her link with David which meant a lot.

She would miss Selina and the calculated chaos that was her life, but there would be other friends and there was always Gareth.

She was not sure how she felt about Gareth.

Chapter Eleven

IF GARETH MEANT nothing to her, if he was just the friend she told Selina he was, then why did she keep thinking about him?

Next day she went over the conversation with Selina. She had made the mistake somewhere along the line of mentioning Gareth which led to question after question including the telling one 'what colour are his eyes?' Francesca avoided answering that, although, curiously enough, she did remember exactly what colour they were which must mean something.

'What *is* this?' she had asked at last. 'The Spanish Inquisition?'

'Oh come on, I'm just interested that's all. You're the only person that I can talk to about silly little things like this. Bethany is far too young and impressionable and, dare I say it, a bit puritanical.'

'That's been said about me.' Francesca laughed.

Selina gave her a shrewd look. 'Deny it all you will, but I can tell that this Gareth chap has made quite an impression on you.'

'He's just a friend,' she exclaimed in a flurry as she caught the knowing expression in Selina's eyes. 'For heaven's sake, I'm not looking for another man. I've only just lost David.'

'I know that. I'm just trying to cheer you up, darling, by

talking a load of nonsense, but isn't it great to know you've obviously still got it if another man fancies you? Believe me, it's the one thing that keeps us ladies going and a little light-hearted flirtation never did any harm to anybody.'

It worried her that, subconsciously, she might have been doing just that but then he was the sort of guy who just invited it. He was good looking enough to be pleasurable on the eye without any of that cocky awareness that some handsome men have. Even Professor Rosemary Wetherall had not been averse to casting twinkling glances at him. Next time she met him, she would be much more circumspect so that if he did have any ideas he would forget them.

The timing was all wrong.

If she had met him before David, then it might well have been a different story.

After a hectic time in London, she was back in Devon, pro-foundly relieved to be back, and getting ready for the Sandersons' dinner party. She had had a busy day, having to rush off a belated birthday card to Izzy. The last time she had written to her was a brief note to thank her for the wedding present, but it had been one of many little letters, specially printed thank-you cards, and she recalled that there had been no personal touch which she now regretted. Sometimes she treated Izzy so badly that she wondered quite why she contin-ued to keep the friendship ticking over as she did for her own birthday was earlier in the year and Izzy's card, always a cheerfully rude one, meant she had to reciprocate.

She had meant to put a letter in with the birthday card – a bland one-size-fits-all card with pink roses on the cover - explaining what had happened but in the event she did not have the time to compose one and it hardly seemed the right moment anyway, depressing somebody on their birthday. After she posted it, she realized that excluding David's name after the 'with love from' bit might tell Izzy something for Izzy had put with love from Izzy, Alan, Vicky, Sarah, Jane and Mabel on hers but she was in no mood for an Izzy post-mortem on events. She would get round to telling her, telephoning her maybe and probably meeting her now that they lived closer but she was in no great hurry.

Izzy was a face from the past and a constant reminder of something she had no wish to be reminded of. She put it out of her mind, terribly busy as she was with the whole house-purchase business which was proving to be something of a nightmare. It was going through, although it was subject to slowing down procedures that seemed to dog the local solicitors. Francesca's solicitor was a woman, Ms Joanna J. Jennings of Cooper & Franklin whose offices were in a splendid white-fronted building on the Plymouth road. On the telephone during the initial enquiry Ms Jennings had sounded suitably brisk and business-like and her no-nonsense tone had impressed Francesca. She imagined for some reason a small jolly lady in her fifties, rather plump but the reality was a little different.

In the flesh, Ms Jennings was tall and slender and considerably younger than fifty. She had a severe bob so perfect it might have been a wig, sharp features, and a penchant for brightly tailored jackets and unfortunately she had just broken her leg skiing in Colorado. Whilst Francesca had some sympathy with her predicament she could not help feeling annoyed that she had jetted off on holiday when she ought to have been dealing with the reports from the surveyor and the land registry and goodness know who else. All the reports were sitting on her desk and because the fracture was a tricky one and in addition there was some problem with the medical insurance, Francesca did not feel she could be as huffy as she wanted to be. Nobody seemed to have heard of the word delegation in that office and Selina, when she heard the reason for the hold-up, said that she should tell the woman to bung in some pain-killers and get her arse into the office a.s.a.p.

But then Selina would say that, Selina had been known to struggle into the office on the very verge of pneumonia and had been dealing with paperwork at home the day after delivering each of her children. So the unfortunate Ms Jennings got short shrift from her.

On top of that, the Sandersons' solicitor was a certain much loved local man Edwin Northcup, an old dodderer with a name and disposition straight out of a Dickens novel. Unwilling to bow out of the business, he was about eighty and he was just out of hospital after suffering a perforated ulcer so it had to be said that they had been extremely unfortunate in their choice of professionals. So, for the moment, Francesca was renting a furnished flat above the delicatessen on the high street on a short-term lease which she hoped would be sufficient to see her through and this evening she was in the tiny bedroom trying to decide what to wear for the dinner party.

Pamela had issued the invitation and it was not one she felt she could refuse but she was uneasy about the wisdom of accepting it in the first place wondering just what the rules of engagement were. Ought she, the buyer, to be seen to be fraternising with the vendors? She had decided to accept anyway if for no other reason than she wanted to see the house again.

The two parties were sitting, pens poised, all ready for the final signatures when their two scintillating solicitors could get their fingers out so it was just a waiting game but, with both of them anxious to get moving, nothing could possibly go wrong.

Could it?

Reminded of what had gone wrong before with David staging the supreme sacrifice to avoid signing on the dotted line, she was not so sure.

'These damned solicitors,' Pamela Sanderson said, greeting Francesca with a kiss on both cheeks and drawing her into the hall. 'Aren't they so annoying? Richard has been tearing his hair out.' She smiled as she added. 'Figuratively speaking of course.'

Francesca had left her umbrella in the porch, but in the short dash from her flat she felt a bit damp round the ankles in the sudden torrential downpour, peep-toe shoes not being ideal wet weather wear.

'Oh you poor girl. Look at you. You're drenched. You should have driven round.'

Francesca laughed. 'Much too lazy. I only live five minutes away.'

'That's no excuse. I drive *everywhere*, dear. Isn't all this house business taking an age? The good news is that Mr Northcup has just come up trumps and says we should be able to complete by the 12th so you can move in as soon as you like after that. Now you mustn't worry about us. We can move out at a moment's notice because all our furniture is going into storage before we ship it over. I can't wait to get to France,' she said, pausing for breath and taking Francesca's black pashmina from her. 'The weather's gone off, hasn't it? I suppose that's the summer gone unless it perks up again. At least you know where you are in the south of France. It's glorious sunshine all summer long aside from the occasional thunderstorms which are marvellous too in their way.'

'Whereabouts are you moving to in France? Gareth did say but I've forgotten.'

'The Riviera near Nice. Do you know it? The views from our terrace are just outstanding. Blue sea, blue sky, heavenly scents. I can't wait.'

'It sounds lovely.'

'Oh, here's Richard. Francesca's here, darling.'

'Francesca, how nice to see you. Looking lovely as usual.' Her husband appeared, beaming. He was a portly, bald-headed gentleman, several inches shorter than his wife. He was dressed in a formal fashion with a dark suit, white shirt and bow tie. 'Come on through. We wondered whether to light the fire, but we couldn't bring ourselves to do it, not in July. Bloody awful weather, isn't it? Gareth says he's very nearly been blown off the cliff several times. Mind you, the sea over there is a sight to behold when it's like this. Did Pamela tell you Northcup's given us a date?'

'Date?'

'For the move.'

'Of course.' She cursed herself for her lack of attention. Sometimes these days she felt she was on another planet and people must think her very dim. She smiled at Richard, liking him. He and Pamela were two of a kind.

'12th July, but don't hold your breath,' he went on cheerfully. 'I'm not sure we should be doing this, meeting socially. Is it a bit off I ask myself? Don't breathe a word to Northcup. Officious old soul. If he knew we were doing this, meeting behind his back, he'd have another coronary.'

'It was an ulcer, darling.' Pamela fussed around at the drinks cabinet. 'Will you have a dry sherry or would you prefer something else?'

Francesca could not plead she was driving and rather than

cause a fuss accepted the sherry Pamela seemed keen for her to have. She sipped it gingerly and a morsel from a plate of nibbles. Knowing that Pamela had a vast wardrobe and liked to dress up, Francesca had opted for a knee-length dress in oyster silk. Pamela's dress sense straddled a dangerous line, her lustrous long blonde hair à la Marilyn Monroe and the voluptuous figure a hindrance to the elegant image she strived to achieve.

Francesca knew exactly what David would have said about the delightful Pamela and the thought made her smile. She was a sparkling tonic of a lady and would certainly light up the Riviera.

'Full circle,' Pamela said happily, sitting down with her glass. 'The house is coming full circle. Isn't that wonderful? Do you think it knows?'

'Are you kidding?' Richard laughed. 'Excuse me, Francesca, but doesn't my lovely wife talk a lot of bullshit.'

'Language, Richard. I may be used to you, but Francesca's not.'

'It's all right.' Francesca laughed too, although Richard did pull an apologetic face. 'Perhaps it does know.'

'You're not vegetarian or vegan or gluten-free or whatever, are you?' Pamela asked with a sudden squeal. 'Oh my gracious me, I forgot to ask. Please say you're not.'

'Thank goodness for that,' Richard said as she reassured them. 'She's done venison parcels. Freshly shot deer from the farm shop.'

'Humanely dealt with,' Pamela said hastily. 'The poor darling wouldn't have known what had hit it so you needn't worry and it's been hanging ever since. It should be beautifully tender.'

'Lovely.' Francesca smiled although it was gritting teeth time because venison was her least favourite meat.

'With new potatoes, braised leeks and swede and carrot puree,' Pamela rhymed off the menu. 'And for dessert, I've done lime and ginger cheesecake or peach and almond strudel with clotted cream of course. We're having no nonsense with calorie counting tonight, not that you need to worry, Francesca.'

'She's been in the kitchen all day long practising for when we move to France,' Richard said. 'Pamela's going to spend her time cooking delicious meals, shopping in the local market, quilting and what have you and I'm going to sit around doing absolutely nothing.'

'That's what he thinks, Francesca. I must show you a picture of the new house. We have a pool. Isn't that marvellous? I'll just go and get it.'

The bell rang as Pamela returned and handing Francesca the pictures, she jumped up, smoothing the skirt of her dress. 'That will be Gareth,' she said. 'I did mention that he was coming along, didn't I?'

'No. You didn't.'

'Oh sorry. I wasn't being secretive.'

Wasn't she? Francesca asked herself.

With Richard momentarily distracted and Pamela out in the hall, Francesca took a moment to fish in her bag and hastily check her lipstick.

Lilac House still had the faint feel of a B&B as they ate their meal in the dining-room where Francesca, as a guest, had breakfasted not so long ago. Pamela was a charming attentive hostess if a little obsessed by the recent world cruise which she and Richard had enjoyed with the benefit of their stateroom with balcony. After all, what was the point forking out money for a cruise, she said, if all you could afford was a broom cupboard somewhere in the depths of the ship?

'We thought we would go the whole hog. After all, it's only money,' Richard explained, just a shade defensively. 'We have no children and, you never know, either one of us could have a heart attack and drop dead tomorrow. Oh God, sorry, I forgot about....'

The silence was suddenly painful, Pamela springing into action after a shocked moment, but not before she shot her husband an irritated glance.

'It's all right,' Francesca said quickly, seeing his embarrassment and glossing over it. 'Not to worry. Honestly it doesn't matter.'

The main course was very good, the food elegantly arranged on fashionably square plates, the presentation worthy of a TV chef, little towers of venison and vegetables tastefully surrounded by ... well, whatever it was Francesca decided it was best not to refer to it as gravy.

As Pamela fussed around, she exchanged a small smile with Gareth who seemed thoroughly at ease which was in direct contrast to her own state of mind. He had made an effort tonight, wearing shiny leather shoes, smart trousers and a pale blue shirt, but no jacket or tie.

Richard, his earlier slip-up clearly uppermost in his mind, was very careful not to refer in any way to her late husband, but Gareth had no such qualms and brought the conversation round to it by saying that it was great for her to have a big project to deal with.

'I heard somewhere that it helps the grieving process if you have something to do, and there's nothing quite like doing up a house,' he said. 'Getting stuck into this will really help.'

Pamela gave him an annoyed look, irritated on two counts; firstly that he had brought up the subject at all and secondly that he was suggesting that the house needed a major gutting. But, she was an accomplished hostess, and deftly changed the subject back to France.

'Although I am so thrilled to be going abroad I shall miss being here,' she said. 'It's so wonderful to step outside your door almost straight onto the moor. I can remember having some lovely leisurely walks.'

'When?' Richard smiled fondly at her. 'I can count the number of times you have been for a walk on the moor.'

'Yes, well …' she sighed. 'To be honest, unless it's brilliantly sunny I do find it a tad depressing. Miles and miles of grass and bracken and then if the mist does come down you are instantly reminded of Sherlock Holmes and that hound.'

'I love it,' Francesca said, leaping to its defence, looking round at them, but particularly at Gareth. 'You are quite right, though, the mists can be frightening. It was a no go area for us in bad weather. When I was little we used to have picnics in summer. Me and my mother and my brother.'

'Oh, you have a brother? What's his name? What does he do?'

Pamela was waiting for an answer but it was Gareth who picked up on her hesitation, quickly carrying on the conversation. 'I love the moor too, but I probably love my walks along the cliff more because of the sea. You must come over to my place,' he added, looking at Francesca. 'Bring your walking boots.'

'Walking boots?' Pamela laughed. 'She doesn't have any. Do you, Francesca? And if she's anything like me she won't be able to walk in the wretched things. Just get yourself some trainers, Francesca, and have done with it.'

'I'd love to do some proper walking, but I'm very rusty.' She addressed her reply firmly towards Gareth. 'You can't really count an amble round the park in the city, can you?'

'No worries. I'll break you in gently.'

'Remind me, isn't Tintagel all about King Arthur?'

'Indeed. Do you know the story?'

'The *fable*,' Pamela corrected him with a smile.

'He's reputed to have been born on Tintagel Island in the castle there. And just below on Castle Beach you can see Merlin's Cave. Great stuff.'

'If you believe all that nonsense,' Pamela sniffed.

'It's just a short hop from Boscastle,' Gareth said, ignoring her rather pointedly after her last remark.

'Isn't that where they had that terrible flood?'

'Yes but they've put it all behind them. Cornish folk are resilient to say the least. The last time I saw it the river was no more than a trickle. It's difficult to imagine how awful it was on that day.'

'Poor souls.' Pamela sighed. 'I can't imagine anything worse than having your home flooded. I don't like the sea. In fact, I'm frightened of it.'

Richard laughed. 'And there speaks a woman who's just been on a round the world cruise. Now, when we've been dashed about on all the oceans of the world you tell me you're frightened of the sea.'

'That's different. You are perfectly safe on a liner that size.'

'Remember the Titanic,' Richard said, a twinkle in his eye as Pamela went out to get the cheese and biscuits. 'To be honest,' he said quietly when she was out of the room. 'It did get a bit hairy when we had storms and let's face it you can't go around the world without hitting a few. We hit a particularly bad one in the Indian Ocean. Pamela was as white as a sheet, prone on her bed the whole day stuffed with sea sickness pills. I'm lucky. I had the dining-room to myself. It can pitch and toss all it likes and it doesn't bother me. But I tell you, those waves were something to behold. Fantastic but bloody terrifying.'

Pamela returned with an oval tray filled with tiny crackers, bunches of mixed grapes and various cheeses.

'Do help yourselves.'

'That's what I like about the sea,' Gareth said, smiling gently. 'It's moody and it changes colour with its moods. If I had any talent as a painter, I would be in my element. My study in the cottage has this fantastic view.'

'Oh yes,' Pamela said. 'He's not exaggerating. Gareth has this wonderful cottage, Francesca.'

'I thought you lived in a caravan.'

'I do, but I own the cottage,' he said. 'During the summer I live in a caravan in the field next door and let the cottage out to visitors. It's purely a financial arrangement. I wouldn't do it if I didn't have to.'

'Now, Gareth, you know you love living in your caravan,' Pamela chided him gently.

'I suppose I do, but letting out the cottage helps with the mortgage and I'm always glad to move back in winter. I like the sea in winter.'

'Gareth does have creative talents, but he's far too modest,' Pamela said. 'It may not be painting but he writes. Tell her about your books, Gareth.'

'No, no. I would bore her to death,' he said, displaying what seemed to Francesca to be a genuine shyness at the prospect, persuaded eventually by a persistent Pamela. 'It's nothing very exciting. I write technical manuals designed mainly for students offering practical approaches and solutions to business problems. That's it in a nutshell. There ...' he smiled. 'Now I *have* bored you rigid.'

'Technical or not, they are good,' Richard broke in. 'Pamela's right. Gareth is too modest. He was a big player in that field for a long time. What you might call a high flyer. Isn't that so, Gareth?'

'I hate that expression, but I enjoyed it while it lasted,' he said but Francesca could tell he was becoming irritated at the way the conversation was heading. 'Now I'm happy to leave it to others. As for the books, well they are text books for a limited audience. I'm not going to top the best seller list.'

'Hardly.' Pamela laughed. 'Why don't you turn your hand to fiction, Gareth? Write something sexy and exciting set in the business world instead of dreary technical stuff?'

'Thanks for that, Pamela. I take it you won't be wanting a signed copy of my new one?' Gareth asked with a grin, not the least put out by her frankness.

Francesca relaxed, enjoying the banter between old friends, although it reminded her of the dinner parties with David when he held court. Nobody seemed to notice how quiet she was and she found her mind drifting, looking round the room and thinking how she would decorate and furnish it once the Sandersons had removed their furniture.

She could not wait to get her hands on it.

Gareth who had left his car parked more conveniently in town walked her back to her flat.

The rain had stopped and it smelt clean and fresh, the night air cool, the streets glistening.

'I've never met a real life writer before,' she said, teasing him. 'You've been hiding your light under a bushel.'

'Don't you start.' He smiled a little. 'But it's not easy. I'll have you know the dreary, technical stuff as Pamela puts it is very difficult to get across in a simple easy-to-read style. I remember struggling through some stuffy old text books when I was studying and vowing to write one myself one day. It may not be overly exciting, but I do try my best.'

'Don't you mind people living in your cottage?' she asked, changing the subject as she decided enough was enough and he was becoming bored with it. 'Isn't it a bit risky having strangers staying in your home?'

'I admit I wouldn't choose to do it if I didn't have to. I couldn't do what Pamela and Richard did, run a B&B.'

'You knock up a good breakfast.'

'Thanks.' He seemed pleased at that. 'I decided to just provide the accommodation and my guests do all their own catering. I do it for the money because financially it helps a lot. I don't make much from the books although I do top it up with articles and commissioned work sometimes for trade magazines. The truth is I can't rely on it so I can't afford to be too precious about the cottage. I've furnished it simply so it's no big deal if somebody breaks the odd vase. Being on my own it's no problem camping out in the caravan during the summer. Quite the reverse in fact. If I had a family, it would be different of course.'

'I suppose that's the upside of being alone. You can do exactly as you like and at least you have nobody to blame but yourself for your decisions. Sometimes I can't believe that I've bought a house, just like that.'

'What did it feel like tonight being back there?'

'Odd. But I hope I've done the right thing. I wonder what David would have made of it. I suppose he would have wanted me to go up to Yorkshire and continue his dream but it was impossible without him.' She smiled a little, surprised that she could talk about David to this man without embarrassment. 'My friend Selina from London thinks I'm mad.'

'Will she come to see you?'

'I doubt it. She says it's too far.'

'That is the penalty of moving to the sticks. My friends said exactly the same thing. They said it would drive me nuts, that I would miss being near the smart cafés and bars not to mention the theatre. You did mean it, I hope, when you said you would like to come over to see my place?'

'Of course. I'd love to. I'll have things to do as soon as I get my hands on the key but I'll be along the moment I get myself settled in.'

He reached for his wallet, fished out a card. 'My number,' he said. 'Gareth Bailey at your beck and call, day or night.'

'Thanks.'

There was an awkward moment as he prepared to leave. Out of politeness, she wondered if she should invite him in for a coffee, but felt the offer might be misconstrued. Seeing him hesitate, Francesca took charge, she reached up and kissed him on the cheek. 'Goodnight and thanks again,' she said.

'Goodnight Francesca. Promise me you'll keep in touch.'

She closed the door on him, leaning against it a moment, finding herself smiling before letting out a slow deep breath and listening to his footsteps going away.

Chapter Twelve

FRANCESCA WAS FINALLY living back at Lilac House.

Pamela and Richard had looked after the house and the survey had revealed no major problems and so the changes she was making were purely cosmetic. It did involve a lot of painting and decorating though, and, following Pamela's recommendation, she chose a local man who did a superb job leaving Francesca time to concentrate on the prettier aspects such as choosing new carpets and fabrics for the curtains. One of the first things she did though, was to remove the carpet from the hall when she was delighted to see that the lovely tiled floor was undamaged if a little dusty. She spent a whole afternoon on her knees cleaning and polishing it and although it left her with aching arms that was nothing compared to the sense of achievement.

She had not completely finished, but after weeks of hard work and having the decorators – nice as they were – constantly under her feet and in her kitchen swilling mugs of tea, she decided on a break before tackling the remainder. She wanted the bliss of being alone again.

She chose a bedroom at the back of the house as her own, leaving what was considered to be the master bedroom with its ensuite bathroom and connecting room for other use. For her room, she chose a calming lavender colour for the scheme with some pretty feminine touches and, with the garden coming along in leaps and bounds under the gardener's guiding hand she was delighted to fling open the curtains in the morning and gaze out.

Francesca chose a bright sunny day to visit Gareth.

Without the benefit of a navigator, satellite or human, she could hear his scarily detailed instructions as she drove, the problems only arising once she actually got herself to Tintagel. At the very last she found she was looking out very unscientifically for a big oak tree sited just before his turn. Blink and you'll miss it, Gareth had told her all this in his cheerful phone call.

Predictably, with the car following practically stuck to her back bumper, she did miss the turn and had to drive on a while before being forced to do an awkward goodness-knows-how-many point turn onto the grass verge before retracing her steps. She needed a satnav she reflected although having experienced Selina's version and the arguments that lady had with it, ignoring it half the time determined it seemed to get the better of the woman's sure-fire instructions, she was not convinced it would help.

Gareth was not joking about the condition of the lane.

The surface was pitted and she drove carefully round the potholes fearing grave damage to the car's underbelly. The caravan was in a field off the end of the lane, the black and white Cornish flag flying by the entrance, and she pulled up, getting out and stretching her legs, wondering which of the ten or so caravans was his. A stiff coastal breeze caught her hair, whipping it into frenzy and the saltiness of the sea was at once on her lips, the sound of surf pounding away in the distance.

She saw Gareth emerging from one of the caravans, surprised at how pleased she was to see him. The site was not too large or obtrusive, the small block of caravans discreetly positioned amongst banks of shrubs.

'Hi there. Nice to see you.' He greeted her with a hug and a quick kiss on the cheek. 'Find it all right?'

'No problem.'

'Good. Most people miss the entrance first time. Come and see the cottage first,' he told her. 'Being Friday it's change-over day so the cleaner will be in but I'd like you to see it.'

'I'm looking forward to it.'

He was no gardener and he thought his guests were more interested anyway in having somewhere to park their vehicles so he had turned the front garden over to paving. There was room for three cars if they jiggled about a bit.

'In any case, it's a fool's errand trying to keep up a garden in this position,' he had said. 'It's far too windy and there's too much salt in the air for most plants.'

'Pity,' she remarked for it would have been so much prettier than the barren concrete area, but she saw his point. This was business and he was quite right about what guests would appreciate.

'Come on in,' he said, pushing at the door and yelling it was only him.

'Mind the Hoover, Mr Bailey. He's in the sitting-room right by the door,' the cleaner called out as they entered.

Francesca smiled. She had almost forgotten about the lovely eccentricity of this region in crediting *things* with a male or female gender.

Entering the sitting room, they obligingly stepped over the cable as *he* was plugged in ready for the off. The cleaner was busy in the kitchen sorting out the bed linen. She smiled at

Francesca as Gareth introduced her, telling him that last week's guests had left the house in a tidy state.

'It makes a change I can tell you. I don't know how some of these people live back home. Sometimes ...' she looked at Francesca, shook her head. 'I could tell you some tales, Mrs Porter. The week before last I came in and I couldn't believe the state of the place. They had left plates and half eaten take-aways all over the lounge and there was tomato ketchup on the sofa. I had a right old job getting rid of that and in the bath-room ... well, you'd think there had been a murder. She left a note to say one of the kids had had a nosebleed. I hope that's all it was. Have you had a long drive?'

'I live over in Devon. It was about an hour.'

'Right. Very nice too.' She looked as if she was about to launch into another question but Gareth put pay to that, placing his hand in the small of Francesca's back, guiding her away, exchanging a smile with her as they went up the narrow staircase.

His study was the only room he shut off, he told her, as he unlocked the door. His guests had the use of the living area, the three bedrooms, bathroom and kitchen but he preferred that they did not come into this room which was a pity because it had the very best view.

'I keep all my papers in here, things I need for researching my book, bills – that sort of thing – so I don't want people snoop-ing,' he explained as she stared, entranced, out of the window.

When he talked about a cottage, she had formed an impres-sion of a small cramped place with low-beamed ceilings – this was nothing like that. It was in fact rather large, almost as big as her house. This room was simply furnished with a modern desk, filing cabinet and shelves stacked with books. A male room with no fripperies whatsoever but she liked the large old rug covering the wooden floor and the big comfortable looking red leather chesterfield.

Having taken in the room briefly, she was having difficulty tearing her eyes away from the view from the window.

'Are you booked for the rest of the summer?'

He nodded. 'I'm booked solid until September. There are people from Wales due later today and next week a family of six from East Devon. I hope the weather's nice for them. I feel sort of responsible. Now … are you ready for that walk or would you like a drink first?' He glanced down at her shoes, sparklingly white brand new sturdy trainers with ridiculously long laces and smiled. 'I see you took Pamela's remarks to heart.'

Gareth was worryingly wearing proper walking boots and thick socks. He was also being evasive as to how far they were going to walk, which was even more worrying.

'Watch the mud by the gate,' he said. 'I wouldn't like you to get your new shoes dirty.'

Francesca glanced sharply at him, suspecting sarcasm, but his face gave nothing away. She walked beside him firmly, matching him stride for stride. Well, not quite but good enough. She had the feeling he was testing her out and she could feel her hackles rising determined not to ask him to slow down even if she was breathing her last. To her annoyance but hardly her surprise, one of her socks was getting bunched up in her shoe just as it used to do when she was a child.

Some things never change.

They headed smartly off down a lane much too narrow for cars with high banked-up hedges on either side moving towards the sound and smell of the sea. It was quiet, the sort of quiet you only get in places like this. It made her realize that city folk never really experience this sort of sizzling silence and, if you live life at a constant buzz like Selina, silence and solitude serve not to make you happy, but nervous.

The pace he was setting was cracking and she was too warm already taking off her casual jacket and tying it round her waist. Gareth had stopped up ahead, rather elaborately waiting for her but she needed to pause for a breather, trying to disguise that fact by rooting around in her bag for her sunglasses. She had packed everything else in her bag, any manner of useless items such as eyeliner for heaven's sake, but no sunglasses so she would just have to squint and make the best of it.

Within minutes of crossing over a field full of wild flowers, they walked directly into the view from the study window and at close quarters with a h ly combination of ocean and grassy smells it was even more enchanting.

'Would you just look at that?' Gareth said drawing to a halt beside her, aware that this was the first time she had experienced a view that was so very familiar to him. 'What do you make of that?'

She shielded her eyes with her hand and looked.

No words were adequate. As far as views were concerned this one could take its place with any other in the world. The wonderful thing was that another layer of grief peeled away and lifted off her as she looked at it, at the sheer wonder of nature, mind boggling in its ragged beauty as she looked at the sea tumbling about far below the cliffs, a clear turquoise sea more in keeping with Pamela's Mediterranean dream than this cooler ocean. The waves were tumbling in, frothy-edged like lace on a nightgown, breaking on the shore, and then as if taking a breath pausing before slipping back. The cliffs to one side of the beach looked sheer, but they were climbable, Gareth

informed her, with plenty of handholds amongst the rock and
vegetation.

'Have you climbed them?'

'No. That's not for me. I'm not into rock climbing.'

'Me neither,' she said, shuddering at the very idea.

'We'll walk up to the headland over there if you're up for it,'
Gareth said. 'Then we can sit down and have a rest.'

'I shan't need a rest,' Francesca assured him, irked again
that he seemed to think she was some sort of frail little old
lady. True, in recent years she was a stranger to walking, other
then the few steps necessary to get her from car to wherever
she was going, but she would show him that she could still do
it. She crouched down and adjusted the offending sock before
following him.

To get to the headland they had to go up and over the
gentler slopes of the cliff, although in this context that
seemed a misnomer. There were some steps cut into the hill
for the non-climbing members of the public which were supposed to make it easier, but somehow made it worse. It was
like climbing up a broken down escalator, a very long one,
some of the steps depressingly steep, and Gareth was striding
along, slowing from time to time to allow her – gasping – to
catch up.

This was proving to be a good deal more difficult than she
had expected.

'Want a hand?' He held out his hand as they neared the top
but she shook him away, determined to do it on her own, even
though by now her knees were very nearly giving way. She had
never before been so glad to see a bench and sink onto it, all
pretence of being fit gone. Gareth produced a bottle of mineral
water and passed it over.

'Are you all right?' he asked and she thought she detected

amusement in his voice which was a bit rich considering she might be close to pegging out. She could not speak yet, merely nod as if she did this sort of thing every day. Eventually, she was well enough to take a welcome sip of water.

'Thanks.'

'Sorry, I should have known. I wasn't intending to test you out.'

'Weren't you?'

'No. On second thoughts it is a bit challenging for a beginner. We should have stuck to the lower walk.'

She couldn't rid herself of the feeling as she glanced at him that, despite his protestations he had done it deliberately, the little smile he was trying hard to conceal the giveaway.

'OK. You win, Gareth Bailey. I need to get fitter,' she admitted once she got her breath back. 'What can you expect? I've been practically living in my car for the last few years and when I was working there was never any time for the gym.'

'Don't worry. You're young and you're not carrying any excess weight so you will soon get fit living round here. You should get yourself a dog, take it for walks.'

'I'd like that,' she said. David had intended to get dogs when they moved, two black Labradors to complete his new image of country squire. 'Do you have one?'

'I'm between dogs,' he said. 'But yes, I will get another. How's the house coming along?'

'Fine. You must come for dinner when it's finished,' she said, lifting her face to the sun feeling exhilarated now that they had done the climb. Below them, the sea whooshed a little more angrily against the rocks and there were just a few visitors strolling along the path below.

Gareth said it would be busy in Tintagel itself, privately dismissing the King Arthur thing as pure hype although the visitors it brought to the town were very welcome – its life blood in fact.

'Don't knock it then,' Francesca told him. 'The locals won't like that.'

'I don't knock it. I never do that. I'm only telling you. And, however sceptical you might be, however much you sneer at it, there is something about it that does pull you in. There's a magical feel, no two ways about it. I defy anybody not to feel something is there.'

'Now you're back tracking,' she said, teasing him and was surprised to see a slow flush cover his cheeks.

'Francesca …?'

'What?' she said, more sharply than she intended, but there was something in his tone that worried her. She hoped he wasn't going to make a move, declare his undying love, something like that, because that sort of thing when she was not ready for it might push the friendship one step too far.

'I have to tell you something about myself, Francesca, something that you're not going to like one little bit,' he said, inching away slightly as if they had been sitting very cosily together which they had not for her overstuffed bag was very firmly in between them. 'I think before things go any further, you should know something about me.'

'You're married,' she said at once, jumping in with the obvious. 'It's OK. I don't have any designs on you, Gareth,' she went on hastily. 'I've just lost my husband for goodness sake. Give me a break, please.'

'I'm not married and I know that you've just lost your husband, but I want to be straight with you and it's best sometimes to come out with these things at the beginning. Just in case …'

'Just in case what?' she bristled. 'Forget it, whatever it is. I'll

forgive you unless it's something awful of course. I can't believe
you're about to confess that you've committed a murder and
got away with it or that you've just served a long stretch in
prison.' She tried a laugh, but it was hollow. 'Can't we just go
on for a while as we are, Gareth? I haven't got many friends
here, not yet, and I want us to stay friends, just friends. I don't
need any complications.'

There. It was said and she couldn't make it any clearer, could
she?

'I'm sorry, Francesca, I know it's too soon and I know you're
in pain. I can see it in your face and I wish I could help.'

'You can't,' she said abruptly.

'But I can. When you lose somebody, you need people around
you, people you can trust. Don't go into a shell, Francesca.
That's not good and it won't help.'

'I'm not going into a shell. If you give me a chance I'm
coming out of it. Don't push me. Perhaps we need to get one
thing clear. I'm not ready for another relationship if that's what
you're hinting at.' She could feel her face flaming, but she had
looked into his eyes and there was no mistake that he was
starting to think of her as slightly more than a friend. 'I bought
the house and I am doing it up and for the moment that's quite
enough for me.'

'I know. These things take time but you're not going to shut
yourself away for ever, are you? Would he want that?'

'No of course not. And I dare say I will think about it sometime but not yet. Rebound relationships are never any good,
are they? Don't rush me,' she warned, lightly brushing his arm.
'You and I are just friends. That's all. Please don't be offended.
I really appreciate your friendship. I don't want you to walk
away from me. To be honest I feel a bit lonely,' she said, desperate to make amends.

'Fine by me. But even so, I should tell you about this. I don't want secrets between us and if you hang onto a secret long enough it gets harder to tell.'

Oh how true and how little he knew about her.

'Oh for goodness sake, Gareth, you're getting on my nerves now. What is it?' She stood up ready and indeed willing now for the return journey.

'We'll take the longer way down,' he said. 'Can you see the path stretching out over there. We'll head down there. Come on ...'

'No.' She shook off his proffered hand. 'I'm not budging until you tell me. You are not keeping me in suspense a minute longer.'

'OK. Sit down.'

They sat down again, side by side. There was a slight breeze but it was pleasant and warm and Francesca closed her eyes to it, hearing the surf and very aware of Gareth beside her. Whatever it was, whatever was so important to him that he had to make such a big thing of it did not matter. She had formed an instant impression of him when they first met as she had with David and she was rarely wrong. Whatever he had done she could forgive.

Well, almost anything.

'You said you could forgive me almost anything but you hit it on the head, Francesca, when you said you might perhaps not if it was something really awful. Well, it *was* something really awful. I was responsible for killing a young girl.'

On the edge of the cliff, a little too close to the edge for comfort, Francesca watched a gull swoop low as if it was landing before it did a sort of silent change of gear and soared away on the warm sea breeze.

She had to hand it to him.

It was a conversation stopper.

Chapter Thirteen

THEY WERE HOLED up in Gareth's caravan having a coffee. At the last, Francesca had to limp down the lane from the field and when she took off her trainers and socks she had a blister the size of a five pence piece on her foot. After the shock announcement he had clammed up, saying stiffly that they should get back and they had completed the walk in virtual silence other than standing aside to make room for other people, exchanging a few friendly words with them in the time honoured tradition of people in the same boat or, in this case, on the same narrow coastal path.

Once in the caravan, she sat down thankfully on part of the curved seating arrangement rolling up the hem of her trousers as, calmly and efficiently, he administered to her medical needs, soaking her feet in a little bowl of warm water which was utter bliss before patting them dry with a soft fluffy towel and sprinkling them with some medicinal powder.

'Better?'

She nodded, speechless. To her horror, she had felt a vague erotic pull as he carefully and thoughtfully tended to her needs. Womanly awareness reared its head then and she registered that following the energetic little stroll she must look like hell although she was thankful that her legs were freshly smooth and lightly tanned at that so she was not letting the side down in that department. Her hair was all over the place though and she tugged at it ruefully.

'Sorry about that. I never meant you to get a blister. I can see I shall have to break you in a bit more slowly,' he said, washing his hands afterwards at the little sink.

'It's my fault. It was a daft idea to wear new shoes and it was hardly a marathon. I'm not usually such a shrinking violet,' she said, half teasing but annoyed with herself at the same time.

'I know that.'

Having dropped the bombshell on the walk he now infuriatingly seemed in no great hurry to come up with explanations so she had not much option but to wait. A little more comfortable now, she looked round this other place he called home, such a contrast to his lovely cottage.

There seemed to be no shortage of mod cons and it was all very cute in a Lilliputian way and Francesca could see that for a single man it would be perfectly fine to spend the summer here. It might be rather fun at that, back to being a child again, playing at houses. It was all neat and tidy, but that's what she had come to expect of Gareth. David, despite his immaculate personal appearance, had been content to let somebody else tidy up for him, his cleaner and latterly his wife although that had been temporary and she had been working up to sharing the workload in a fairer way.

Another forlorn hope.

'Gareth ...?' Barefoot, she wiggled her toes and, to make it easier for him, avoided eye contact.

He opened a cupboard, reached in and pulled out a packet of shortbread biscuits. 'Want one?'

'No thanks,' she said. It was as if he had never said what he had said up on the edge of the cliff. Her impatience spilled over and she sat up straighter repeating his name in a questioning way.

He took a biscuit, nibbled at it. 'I suppose you want to know the full story?'

'Of course I want to know the whole story.' She managed a brief laugh. 'The suspense is killing me. You can't just spring something like that on me and then let it drop.'

'It happened a few years ago, I was involved in a car accident.' he gave a low whistle as he exhaled. 'The woman, the young girl, in the other car died.'

'Oh. I see.' She let out a sigh. 'I guessed it was an accident but you might have made that clear.'

'Didn't I?'

'No. Although I never thought for a moment you had actually murdered her.'

He did not laugh. 'No, but she ended up dead. I killed her, Francesca. I killed her just as much as if I had strangled her.'

'That's not true unless you deliberately ran into her or you were drunk at the time and if that was the case you would have gone to prison.' She paused, looked up. 'That didn't happen, did it? '

'No. I was stone cold sober and the verdict was accidental death.'

'So how can you say you were responsible?'

'You weren't at the inquest. You didn't see the state her parents were in. You didn't see the way her mother looked at me. I'll never forget that look. She blamed me, I could tell.'

'Well she was wrong to blame you. It wasn't your fault. When something like that happens I know it's hard but you have to try to forget,' she said, knowing she was a fine one to be telling him this. 'When accidents happen, people always have to look for somebody to blame. That's the way it is and …' she stopped, seeing that he was not listening and she knew that he was remembering instead, recalling the incident as vividly as she recalled James's. 'What happened? You can tell me.'

'It started out as an ordinary day.'

'They always do,' she said, remembering the three of them wandering down to the river, James bounding ahead, she and Izzy drifting along behind, chatting about this and that.

'I wouldn't care but I'd only gone out in the car to take some reference books back to the library. They weren't even due back for God's sake. They could easily have waited a few days. I didn't need to be out on the road. And, if I hadn't been out on the road then she wouldn't have hit me. Would she?'

She kept quiet. No, but there would have been another car to hit but she would let him tell it in his own way.

'She was a learner driver, or rather she'd just passed her test. She was seventeen, Francesca. A child. She was a lovely young girl with all her life before her. Her name was Stephanie.'

'Pretty name,' she said helplessly and uselessly.

'Yes. A pretty name. It was a bad corner, tight, and yes, she came at it badly, too fast, and momentarily she was on the wrong side of the road, my side of the road, but surely I could have done something to avoid her. I could have swerved out of the way onto a grass verge which wouldn't have done me any harm but I didn't and she hit me full on and then bounced off across the road into a tree. She didn't have her seatbelt on either. Oh God, it all happened so fast. I was fine apart from whiplash but she was crushed and trapped and it took an age for them to get her out. The firemen cut her out eventually and got her to hospital but it was already too late. We all knew it was too late.'

Francesca felt a relief surge through her. Good heavens, he

was full of guilt for something that really was not his fault. She, on the other hand, was guilty of something that most certainly *was* her fault. Sitting there in the caravan, she felt that pull of guilt again.

The guilt that was always just a heartbeat away.

It was just another day.

It was the school holidays and they, she and Izzy, were lounging about on the river bank anxious to get a natural tan after some disastrous efforts with the fake stuff. Grensley Bridge had become their place, a perfect spot for an illicit smoke. It was a quiet place even in summer for most people tended to congregate at the better known and easier to get to bridging point up river where there was ample parking and easier access to the moor.

Their plans for the day were in tatters because with Francesca's mother otherwise engaged trying to sell her pots over in Truro, Francesca had been roped into looking after her six year old brother.

'You will keep your eye on him?' her mum asked, ready for the off, her wild red hair pulled up on top of her head in a messy arrangement, a narrow black ribbon anchoring it there more or less. 'You know I don't like to leave him for the whole day but he really would get in the way, bless him, when I'm trying to look professional and everything. Children and business meetings just do not mix. Now, I'll try to be as quick as I can, but I have several appointments and you never know how long they will take. Are you quite sure you'll be OK?'

'Yes, mum.' She reacted in the usual bored teenage way. Honestly why did her mother feel she had to issue pages of instructions whenever she went anywhere. 'For the hundredth time we will be just fine.'

'Don't be cheeky.' She shot her a fond glance. 'He's not to have any sweets. He's had his ration for the week.'

'I know.'

'And you're not to go anywhere near the river. Are you listening, Francesca?'

'Mum ...' she protested. 'As if ...'

'Got to go.' Her mum grinned at her, the last time she was ever to look at her like that, waved a cheery goodbye and with that she was off in a flurry of summery skirt and perfume.

Izzy had been looking after *her* younger brothers since she was eleven and her mum never made such a fuss about it and none of them had come to any harm. Izzy laughed when she told her about her mum's fussing and on the way down to the river, they broke the first rule by stopping at the shop and buying James some sweets, managing to refrain from buying some for themselves because of the constant danger of erupting spots.

Francesca handed over the little bag to the delighted James. 'If Mum asks you're not to tell her. You're not supposed to have them,' she told him.

'And you're not to tell her we've been down to the river either,' Izzy said, grabbing him and squeezing him tight. 'Are you listening, James Blackwell? If you tell then I'll wave my magic wand and make you disappear. Do you promise? Cross your heart and hope to die.'

He squealed until she let him go, but laughed at her before promising not to tell. Standing aside, Francesca's heart ached a little at the easy camaraderie the two of them shared; anybody would think James was Izzy's brother instead of hers.

In fact, although they had missed a shopping trip into Plymouth it was not so bad relaxing here in the sunshine. After all what did they do in town other than prance about and hope to be noticed. They counted the number of looks they got from boys and afterwards they played at being the interesting girls in café thing, spending ages over one hot chocolate or fizzy drink.

Francesca's mother made no secret of the fact that she did not really approve of Izzy thinking her a bit too worldly wise and it was true that Izzy did seem older than her years, but other than saying 'watch that girl, she's trouble,' her mother had not gone so far as to ban Francesca from seeing her. For a girl of sixteen it wouldn't have worked anyway. Izzy was the popular girl whom everybody wanted as their friend and it seemed, for reasons she was hazy about, that she had chosen Francesca.

Izzy had got her started on the smoking. Francesca envied Izzy her chaotic family, her happy go lucky mum, her loving dad and also her carefree attitude to life. Izzy might be the cleverest girl in class, but it was almost certain she was not the one who would get the best grades. Her teachers despaired that she would not fulfil her potential and somehow slip through the cracks in the education system, but she was in the happy position of being put under no pressure from her parents, just told to do the best she could. Francesca knew that, notwithstanding the importance of their exams these days, Izzy was not working at full capacity.

Having to work her own socks off to achieve decent grades, anxious to do well because her mother expected nothing less, Francesca could not understand Izzy's attitude, but as Izzy's sole ambition was to get married and have a horde of children what did it matter? Izzy was more in tune with attitudes of the nineteenth rather than the twentieth century – ambition and a worthwhile career were not a part of her thinking and planning ahead.

Lying on the river-bank, Francesca was enjoying the sun-shine and listening to Izzy's accounts of what she had got up to the previous evening with her boyfriend who was eighteen and already working as a car mechanic. He had promised to give Izzy driving lessons as soon as she was old enough which would not be long. From what Izzy was saying he was giving her lessons of a more intimate nature already.

Francesca doubted it was true. Izzy had a vivid imagination and she suspected that it was just a deliciously exaggerated yarn, but she was not going to challenge her. It was exciting stuff to listen to, true or not.

She looked closely at Izzy finding herself fascinated by the smoky make-up round her eyes. Izzy was enviably curvy; she was just on the right side of plump, with a mass of dark curly hair and her sparkly blue eyes did not really need any enhancement. Francesca experimented a bit with make-up, but her mother said she looked better without it and, although that got her back up, she tended privately to agree.

'And then he kissed me again and off he went,' Izzy finished the tale triumphantly. 'I'm seeing him again next week. He's taking me to the cinema.'

'Lucky you. I can't wait for the next thrilling instalment.'

'Are you being sarcastic?'

'No,' Francesca protested. 'It's like a Mills & Boon story. I want to know what happens in the next chapter.'

'There you go again.'

'What did I say? Honestly, Izzy, you're so touchy.'

'And you're just jealous. You could have a boyfriend if you tried a bit more. You're not bad looking. All you have to do is stop being so snooty. Boys don't like you looking down your nose at them.'

'I'm picky,' she said, not willing to admit that it was the miserable shyness that got in the way. 'There isn't a single boy at school that I fancy.'

'Oh no, they're hopeless. That's why you need an older boy.'

After a moment they both smiled. Their spats never lasted long and were quickly forgotten just like an old married couple. 'But you'll have to watch it,' Francesca went on. 'He's older than you so ...'

'I know. I know.' Izzy blushed at that, cheeks flooding with colour. She might be the cleverest, but she was not the prettiest girl in the class. What she did have though was impressive breasts for her age and a very impish look and a raucous laugh that appealed to the boys. 'That won't happen. I have that all sussed out. I've had a talk with my mum.'

'Have you? Gosh, we don't talk about things like that.'

'She says if I have any sense I'll wait until I'm at least eighteen before I get serious. She was pregnant herself at seventeen and she doesn't want that to happen to me although things have worked out for her, haven't they? They are still soppy about each other. I wouldn't be surprised if she has another baby. She's only really happy when there's a baby round the house.'

Francesca raised herself up to check on James who, having scoffed his sweets, was looking after himself digging about in the sandy grit by the water's edge moving pebbles around with a stick, chattering away to himself. Satisfied he was OK, she lay down again. She knew that, because of the age difference, she would never enjoy the kind of relationship Izzy had with her brothers. The truth was, although she loved James, she could not rid herself of the feeling that he was to blame for her dad leaving home. It was never explained to her, not properly, and because she was only ten she might not have understood in any case. It hurt though, and it still hurt that he had just upped and left and never made any attempt to make contact afterwards. It hadn't been her fault whatever it was and it wasn't fair that he should shut her out of his life so completely. That was men, her mother had explained, they couldn't be trusted, not one of them.

'Frankie ...' she heard her brother's voice calling, but merely raised an arm in acknowledgement. How many times had she told him not to call her that? She hated it for it was her father's pet name for her and she had no idea where James had picked it up because he had never known him.

'Frankie,' Izzy repeated with a laugh. 'I think I'll start calling you that. Francesca's such a mouthful.'

'Thanks a lot. I like it.'

'Stop calling me Izzy then. You can call me Isabel instead.'

'Izzy's OK. You look like an Izzy.'

Izzy frowned. 'I suppose you think your name sounds sophisticated? Aren't names difficult? Hardly anybody I know likes their own name, but then you don't get a say in it, do you? I have a list of my favourites for my own kids.'

'I'm never going to have kids.'

'Where did that come from?'

'I've just been thinking, that's all. I don't want kids. Not ever.'

'You'll change your mind.'

'No, I will not,' Francesca said, shaking her head. 'You forget, Izzy, I was ten when James was born and Mum had a terrible time. She started off at home and you should have heard the screaming before she was carted off. I'm not kidding, we nearly lost both of them. It was touch and go.'

Izzy laughed. 'Oh come on, it's the twentieth century. Women don't die in childbirth these days.'

'Mum nearly did and she was ill for months after. There's no way I'm putting myself through that.' She sighed, remembering how she had practically brought up James on her own with her mum being so out of it. She would spend most of the day in bed and expected Francesca to look after the baby when she got home from school. With her dad gone, what they had done for money during those long months – the first few months of James's life – she had no idea, but they managed, just about, and then, when her mum had recovered a little, she started making the pots again. She thought some money came her mother's way from her father, but her mother clammed up whenever money was mentioned, always maintaining that they had enough to get by on and she wasn't to worry.

'I'm having four babies, two of each,' Izzy said, a dreamy look on her face. 'I might even marry Martin if he asks me.'

'A car mechanic?'

'Why not? You're such a snob. What's wrong with that? He could have his own garage one day.'

'I suppose so,' Francesca said doubtfully. Martin was gritty and good-looking yes but he didn't look very bright although she was not about to tell Izzy that, not when she was obviously half in love with him already.

'I read somewhere that you should get married young and have your kids young so that you can be rid of them by the time you're forty. Then you can do all the things you've always wanted to do.'

They laughed at that, stubbing out their cigarettes in unison and glancing up at the wide blue sky. With the temperature soaring, Izzy started to unbutton her denim shirt, pausing as she caught Francesca's expression.

'It's OK to bathe topless,' she said. 'There's nobody around.'

'There's James,' Francesca said giving her a warning look. 'You shouldn't. Not in front of him.'

'Come off it, he's only a child. You're such a prude.'

Francesca flushed, opening her mouth to protest then deciding not to bother. She had made her point though and, although she looked irritated, Izzy fastened up the buttons again and they settled down, arranging themselves on the dry rough grass, closing their eyes and relishing the sun on their faces.

'It smells like summer,' Francesca said, voice gentle and happy.

'That's because it *is* summer. Sometimes, Francesca, you do talk a lot of crap.'

Neither of them noticed that James had, in the meantime, abandoned his game with the pebbles and stick and had climbed onto the stone parapet of the bridge, the little stone bridge that spanned this stretch of the river and was even now poised like the tightrope walker he had recently seen on television. Arms stretched wide with a big grin on his face, he edged forward towards the centre oblivious to the fact that, if he fell in, he'd only just achieved confident swimming with the aid of armbands.

Below the bridge, the river at that point shelved steeply and was dark and deep, an inky blackness they had often peered into, trying in vain to gauge the depth, the bottom indistinct, but full of tangled weeds.

In Gareth's caravan, resurfacing from the memory, she let out a little gasp of horror and shuddered.

'Are you all right?'

She nodded gathering herself together.

'It wasn't your fault,' she repeated. 'You have nothing to reproach yourself for. I don't know why you think you should tell me because I can't help, Gareth. I wish I could.'

'I know you can't. It's something I've got to live with for the rest of my life. For some reason, it's been on my mind all week. I never talk about it, but I wanted to tell you, Francesca. It put pay to a relationship I had because she couldn't understand why I was letting it get to me. Like you, she kept on saying it was an accident.'

'It *was* for heavens sake. It could happen to any driver.'

'I don't want it to spoil things for us.'

Oh dear, that sounded a little too earnest for her to take in and for a moment, she felt like telling him her story, but the feeling passed for there had been enough confessions for one day. The stupid girl, a new driver going too fast without a seat-belt – well, honestly, sad as it was, she did have it coming.

She escaped the caravan soon after that, declining his invitation to stay. If she stayed for supper it would drag over and the sleeping arrangements in the caravan were a bit too cosy for her liking. In any case he had become morose and she couldn't cope with that. It wasn't fair of him to expect her to. She needed time on her own and the drive back gave her that time. It was disconcerting that Gareth seemed to be relying on her more and more, determined it seemed to take the relationship a step further. It was alarming and astonishing that her body was behaving so treacherously, so soon after David had died, and she wondered what he would say. She worried that she might have ended up in Gareth's bed tonight doing a little consoling and she did not want to have to face the consequences of that in the morning. Good heavens, they were both a mess with enough emotional baggage to fill a carousel at the airport.

There was one important difference.

His guilt was entirely self-inflicted.

Chapter Fourteen

THE VOICE ON the phone was that of a stranger, a woman's voice, pleasant sounding with a northern accent and as soon as she asked if she was speaking to Francesca Porter, Francesca was immediately suspicious of a cold caller. Coming as it did when she was just about to start eating, albeit a salad, she mentally prepared herself for a polite, but firm response.

'I'm not selling anything,' she said quickly before Francesca could end the call. 'And I'm sorry to call you out of the blue, but we've been trying to contact you for some time.' Her laugh was a little forced. 'May I introduce myself? I'm Miss Hannah Williams. I am a senior community liaison officer and I work for a local government agency here in Yorkshire. I can give you a telephone number if you wish to ring it to check my credentials and call me back.'

'You've got it wrong, Miss Williams. We're not moving to Yorkshire any more,' Francesca told her wondering quite why social services should feel the need to be in contact. 'We were in the process of buying a house,' she went on, aware she was in danger of unnecessary explanation. 'But we backed out because my husband died recently.'

'I'm so sorry for your loss,' she said briskly. 'But my call has nothing to do with that. It's your father, Mrs Porter. He requested that we try to locate you.'

'You're not a private detective?'

'Goodness no, although sometimes we have to act like one. Your father is in a nursing home and he's very ill. Let me reassure you that he's being very well cared for. It's a beautiful place outside town with lovely views and an excellent reputation. I visited him recently and he is perfectly happy there.'

'My father?' What Miss Williams was actually saying finally pierced through her muddled mind and she fiddled with the phone cord, missing what the lady was saying next and having to ask her to repeat it. Time, it appeared, was of the essence if she wanted to see her father again.

'Hang on a minute,' she interrupted the lady in full explanatory flow. 'You can't just spring this on me. Are you aware of our circumstances?'

'Yes. He has confided in me. I know there has been an estrangement.'

'Well then, you will know that I haven't seen him since I was ten years old. He left us and never came back,' she said, voice rising. 'He just cut me off completely. I haven't had a birthday card or a Christmas card from him. He never came to my graduation or my marriage ...' she ignored the fact that *nobody* came to that. 'And now you expect me to come up there to hold his hand just because he happens to be dying. I must say he has an almighty nerve.'

'You are angry, Mrs Porter.'

'Damned right I am.' She felt her heart pound, ridiculously annoyed by the sound of this woman's patiently professional voice. How dare she interfere in people's private lives? She had absolutely no business to be doing so.

'Mrs Porter, if you will allow me to continue a moment? This predicament is not as unusual as you might think. It happens all the time. People, family, lose touch for various reasons over the years. Often people in your father's situation feel an over-whelming desire to set things right at the end of their lives before it is too late.' Miss Williams' voice was gentle, but pow-erfully persuasive. Francesca had a vision of a plump friendly face, mid-fifties she thought, soberly dressed and not married, although it could be that she simply used her maiden name at work. Perhaps she was a mother herself, her children grown up by now. She could hear the voice, the pleasant soothing voice, but she was no longer listening.

'Mrs Porter? Are you still there?' the prompt was soft.

'I'm sorry. What were you saying?'

'I was just trying to explain your father's motives. Believe me, in all my experience of this sort of thing it's almost always for the best that you make the effort to see him.'

'Best for whom? For him or me?'

'Both of you.'

'How did you find me?'

'Does it matter? He's kept some sort of track of you over the years so we knew you were working in London and although you're no longer doing that we were able to ascertain your change of name and, via one of your colleagues, your new address.'

'Really?' she was astounded that somehow or other she was still on the radar. For heavens sake couldn't you just choose to disappear in this country? Did you have to be up there on the system so that any old Tom, Dick or Harry or in this case a long lost father could find you? But then she remembered she had informed the office of her new address in case they needed to contact her about any of her previous accounts. However she was a little put out that they had divulged the information to a third party.

Obviously it was too late now.

'Your particulars will be deleted from our database if you wish them to be,' Ms Williams went on, seeming to read her mind. 'So you need not fear that. We are under an obligation to tell your father that we've located you, but we've also had to tell him that he mustn't expect too much either. You are quite at liberty to refuse to see him.'

'Good. Then I refuse.'

'I understand perfectly and I can't force you of course. It's entirely up to you, but I would urge you to think very carefully before you say no. Please give it some consideration. Can I at least give you the details of where he is and a phone number should you change your mind?'

Reluctantly, she took down the details, reiterating belligerently that this didn't mean she was coming up. She would have to think about it.

Replacing the receiver, she looked into the mirror and gave a loud Selina-type curse. After all this time, he thought he could still get round her. After all this time, he expected her to drop everything and rush to his dying bedside.

It took all of five minutes, five seconds even, to make the decision. Rushing upstairs, she quickly packed a bag.

By coincidence, the nursing home was a stone's throw from the house she and David very nearly bought and it took some careful map-reading to avoid driving through the very village. Remembering the time they had visited it, full of excitement, she could not bear to see it again, very likely with the For Sale board resurrected by the wall. Who else would have the nerve to buy what had been a once beautiful but was now sadly dilapidated house? Not many people possessed David's obsession with moving up here at any cost. He was totally unfazed by the thought of extensive and expensive refurbishment, although he would not of course have done any of it himself.

That particular house, on paper anyway, was his idea of perfection or would be when they had paid a fortune out to builders and decorators, whereas for Francesca the very word 'potential' made her heart sink. Potential to her meant living on a building-site and picnicking in one room for months.

'Leave the talking to me,' David had said on the way over. 'We mustn't seem too keen even if we are.'

'I do know that,' she teased him, laughing at his uncharacteristic anxiety. She had decided for the sake of harmony to compromise on the location and David had made a big song and dance about compromising on its central-village position when he would have preferred something more remote. 'I work in advertising,' she reminded him. 'And although you always know straight off what the client is thinking when you come up with a proposal you don't always want to show that you know. You have to develop a poker face.'

'You *used* to work in advertising, darling,' he said, stopping the car in the lane outside to check his watch. It was just off the main street if you could call it that, but it was a happy walking distance from all that the village could offer. It wasn't much. There was a pub and a quaint looking church with steeple. Also surprisingly there was a thriving village shop. A small junior school for the children they would never have. Their appointment to view was for two-thirty and it was now two-forty. 'Let's go,' David went on, climbing out and rushing round to open the passenger door. 'They've had time to sweat.'

'David, you are evil.'

She wished these little memories would stop intruding into her mind, particularly just now when she was about to visit her father. She was dreading it and had told nobody, just leaving a message with the chap who did the Lilac House garden that she would be away up north for a couple of days.

Heading indoors she wondered if he would recognize her. Well, obviously not although even after thirty two years she knew she would recognise him.

She signed her name in a book in the hall and a nurse, fully kitted out in a proper uniform, took her into a side room to have a word. If she was in any way surprised at Francesca's sudden appearance she did not show it.

'How lovely to see you,' she said quietly and without condemnation. 'Please don't worry. Your father is dying, but he looks all right. Have you met death before?'

Met death?

'My husband died in his armchair,' she said, feeling the tears welling up. 'I was clattering about in the kitchen and I didn't hear a thing. I don't know if he cried out for me,' she went on, feeling foolishly she had to explain. 'By the time I went back into the room, he was gone. He was just sitting there and he looked very peaceful. Do you think he cried out for me? It was a heart attack.'

'I doubt it. It was probably over in seconds. I am so sorry.' She sounded genuinely sorry as she picked up a folder and opened it.

Curiously relieved to have her hopes that he had not cried out for her in vain confirmed by a professional, Francesca pushed aside the threat of tears, watching as the nurse consulted the notes.

'Your father was living alone in Ripley when he became ill some months ago. The illness was progressive and he could have opted to stay at home and have private nursing care. He is perfectly lucid and was able to make decisions and he chose to move here. The house was sold and he is funding his care privately. At first we thought he had no family, but lately he started talking about you.'

'Did he? I haven't ... we haven't ...' she stumbled over the words, hoping she wasn't going to make a fool of herself. Have you met death? She couldn't get over the odd expression.

'He has fitted in here very well, although gentlemen are in a minority here. It's mostly ladies.'

'How is he?' Francesca found her mouth dry. She hated it here, hated it that her father was here, hated it that he had had to make all these arrangements on his own. 'Can he speak?'

The nurse nodded. 'Oh yes. He can speak very well but the effort tires him. He had another little stroke the other day but his speech is remarkably unaffected; he took a battering though, and his pulse is weak – it really is just a matter of time although it may be a couple of days yet. He'll be pleased to see you. A few days ago when he was a bit better he talked about you a lot. He showed me a picture of the both of you. Mind you, you were a little girl. You've grown up since then. He is a very interesting man, Mrs Porter. Are you ready?'

Following the nurse up carpeted stairs, a vase of silk flowers on the landing window ledge, she was led down a corridor to a room at the end.

'I'll leave you to it,' she said, having knocked once and opened the door introducing her with a brightly optimistic 'here's your daughter, Mr Blackwell' before turning to Francesca and asking if she would like tea or coffee.

Francesca shook her head, stuck for words as she gazed at the bed where her father lay. The room was small, with a tiny bathroom adjoining, but the view from the window was lovely indeed, a sweep of lawn stretching to the distance with hills beyond. She had come armed with a bunch of flowers and some grapes – quite ridiculous – and she put them on a side-table and went across to the bed.

He seemed very nearly comatose, eyes closed, his breathing steady but shallow, but it was her father, even though his curly dark hair was mostly gone and he was much thinner than she remembered.

All the pent-up anger she felt abated in an instant as she sat down in the chair at the side of the bed and leaned forward, speaking in a voice as determinedly cheery as the nurse's.

'Hello Dad, it's me, it's Frankie,' she said as if she had seen him yesterday.

He stirred, keeping his eyes closed, but moving his hand which she took hold of. He had no grip and she held it gently.

'How long have you lived up here?' she asked softly. 'It's a beautiful part of the world.'

For a moment he was silent and she wondered if she was going to get anything out of him at all but, once he began to speak, the words poured out as if he needed to get it over with as quickly as possible.

'I came up here when I left Devon. I got a job teaching at a school near York. Your mother wanted me to move as far away as possible. I tried my best to keep in touch with you. I sent you cards and letters, poppet,' he said, his voice the same but very low. 'Every birthday, every Christmas. I sent you cash or vouchers until you went to college and then your mother moved and didn't let me have her new address. She told me you had a job in London, but she said I was to stop sending you letters because you didn't want to hear from me.'

She squeezed his hand and said nothing. Just at this moment she hated her mother with a vengeance and she did not like that thought.

'She didn't give the cards to you, did she?' His sigh slipped out and she just held his hand even tighter to let him know that it was so. 'I wondered about that. I wanted to see you, but she threatened to kick up a fuss and I didn't want you caught up in all that. It was bad enough that I'd gone away without your having to deal with all that too.'

'You knew where I worked in London?'

'Yes. But I took heed of what your mother said. I didn't want to pester you and it seemed too late, too many years had passed. I didn't want to upset you, set it all off again. Stupid really. We could have got to know each other again and now it's all too late.'

'Shush. Don't talk. Does it hurt?'

He shook his head. 'No pain,' he said. 'It's peaceful now.'

The coverlet was cream, the sheets white and he looked as if he would be more comfortable propped up a little. She fussed a minute with the pillows, accidentally touching his face as she did so which made him turn his head and open his eyes at last to look at her.

'Frankie. My little Frankie.' He seemed surprised. 'It's you.'

'It's me. I've grown,' she said stupidly.

Her father nodded with appreciation. 'You were a bright little girl. I knew you would get on with or without me. She's dead, you know. Your mother.'

'Yes. It was quick.'

'And the boy? Where is he now?'

How much did he know and was it fair of her to upset him now? A white lie just now was the kindest thing.

'Fine,' she murmured. 'James is just fine.'

'Can I tell you something, darling? Something that I could-n't tell you when you were a little girl?'

'Is it about James?' she asked, anticipating what he was about to say.

He nodded. 'You are old enough now to understand that James is not mine. I could have lived with it, brought him up as my son, but she wouldn't have it. She had fallen out of love. She couldn't have the other chap because he was married and would not leave his wife, but she wanted rid of me and she got rid of me. I wanted to stay, told her I was staying and that was that, but she wouldn't have it.' He tried to laugh, nearly succeeding. 'It was a plot, Frankie. She worked on the mums at school, made them suspicious so that they didn't want me there and, between them they cooked up a plot against me. It was cleverly done. How could I, a lone male, be innocent when they all said I was guilty? It was an exclusive little establishment, proud of its reputation. They gave the headmaster little choice. It was him or me. He called me into his office and offered me the sword.'

'The sword?'

'I'm speaking metaphorically. There wasn't a real sword,' he said and she almost smiled that he felt it necessary to explain what a metaphor was as if she were still a child. 'I was finished, poppet, so I thought I might as well kill myself before they came to do it. Don't you see?' He tried to sit up and she adjusted the pillows again so that he could recline there. His eyes were suddenly sharp just as she remembered them.

'What did they accuse you of?'

'Gross misconduct. Shenanigans with a sixth-former. All lies but they found a girl willing to lie and I knew they would do it if I stood my ground. I couldn't have you caught up in that, not a scandal of that proportion because you know what people say, there's no smoke without fire. It would have always lurked there and you would have suffered because of it, so I did the only thing possible, I resigned before they made it public.'

'Oh Dad, you shouldn't have given in to blackmail. You

should have fought it,' Francesca said. 'If it was all lies then it would have come out in the end.'

'I'm not so sure. By that point your mother hated me.'

'You're tiring yourself,' she said, wanting to reach out to him but caught as always by that family trait of holding back on the emotion.

'If I ever came near you or her again then she would tell you what a complete bastard your father was and I couldn't have that but I might have known she would keep my presents from you so that you would never know that, even though I wasn't there, I was always thinking about you.'

'But you are telling me she had an affair, that James is not yours?'

'Oh yes.'

'Then she hardly behaved like an angel, did she, so why did she want rid of you, Dad? You would have looked after them both. I don't understand.'

There was a short silence and she knew she had tired him, that all this talking, all this getting things off his chest, was wearing him down.

'I don't understand either,' he said at last, voice stronger after the little rest. 'Her mind worked in mysterious ways. Love had turned to hate and even though she couldn't have the other bloke, she didn't want me around any more either. That's it.'

'She could have reasoned with you. There was no need to try to ruin your career.' Francesca smiled gently. 'You shouldn't have let them drive you out. You should have stood up to them.'

'And drag the family name through the mud. Mud sticks. They let me go with a reference and I got another job up here so all was well.'

'Have you been on your own ever since?'

He nodded. 'I managed very well until I fell ill. What about you? Are you all right? She called you Mrs Porter. You're married then?'

She nodded. She could not tell him.

'*Happily* married?'

'Yes. David's a wonderful man. He's a barrister.'

'I'm glad you're happy. Your mother's dead, Frankie, and she can't answer us back. She was a good woman and we must try not to talk ill of her and think too badly of her. She had her reasons, you know, but now that she's gone I had to see you again to set things straight. I want somebody other than the undertakers there at the funeral. It's going to be a simple one at the crematorium. It's over in minutes. Conveyor belt. If you don't specify otherwise they play "All Things Bright and Beautiful".'

'Don't talk like that. You've got ages yet. You'll get better.'

'No I won't. I've left details,' he said. 'And a few bits and pieces. A bit of money for you.'

'I don't need money, Dad.'

There was a knock on the door and a woman with a trolley pushed in.

'Oh, I didn't know you had a visitor, Geoffrey,' she said, a little flustered. 'Is this your lovely daughter you're always telling me about, the one who works in advertising? Lucky there's an extra cup.'

The woman poured the tea, adding two spoons of sugar to her father's.

'He likes it sweet, don't you Geoffrey?' She lowered her voice but not nearly enough. 'Lucky you got here,' she said in a dramatically ill-conceived stage whisper. 'He's pain-free but he only has another day or two, bless him.'

Furious, for didn't the woman, some sort of nursing assistant, realise that hearing was the last sense to go, Francesca refused a cup of tea herself almost pushing her out of the room.

'Bring your husband to see me,' he said and for a brief moment he sounded stronger.

'I will,' she told him at once. 'He's busy in court but I'll see if he can get up to see you.'

'I'd like that. I'd like to congratulate him for making you so happy.' He peered closely at her, dad to daughter, and smiled. 'You look lovely,' he said. 'Do you know, if it weren't for the hair, you look so much like your mother. She was a beautiful woman and I forgive her.'

So, despite it all, despite all the anger and bitterness, in a way he loved her still.

In the event, the couple of days turned into ten long days.

She had made it just in time because by the next day his condition had deteriorated and there was to be no more conversation. Afterwards she obeyed all the instructions he had left and scattered his ashes, like David's, on the moor near Ilkley so maybe in some odd way they did meet each other.

Calm and strangely content, she returned home. She had kept her mobile switched off and there were some messages when she returned home including one from Gareth.

There was no need to broadcast what had happened so she kept it to herself.

Chapter Fifteen

SHE WORRIED THAT the last time she had seen him she had been a little terse with Gareth and that, foolishly, he might have got the wrong impression thinking that what he had told her had changed how she felt about him.

She considered phoning him when she got home but the moment passed. He would get over it and perhaps it was just as well giving her time to get off the slippery slide that had surely been leading her towards some sort of sexual involvement.

It was all much too soon.

And now she had to cope with suddenly finding and immediately losing her father although she felt only relief at that rather than any deep grief. Miss Williams in her infinite wisdom had been right and the decision to go up to see him had been for the best.

She hated the trendy expression but it was true; she had been given the comfort of closure.

Whilst she had been away up north, Gareth had also been away, over in London.

She was glad of the time alone and very busy finishing off things at the house. Small items of furniture she had kept in storage duly arrived and she made trips into Plymouth and Exeter and further a-field to Bristol in search of special items.

At last it was beginning to look and feel like home. She was aiming for a traditional country cottage feel with a certain modern twist and she felt she had succeeded.

David who went for grand with a capital G would hate it.

When Gareth finally arrived at Lilac House he was clutching a bunch of flowers, looking ever so slightly embarrassed in the age-old tradition. His offering was nothing too flamboyant, nothing to suggest a lover's gift. It looked a little like an after-thought, a nice one at that, just some feathery and frothy blue flowers from one of the market stalls. He was not to know that the simplicity of the gift meant more to her than an extrava-gant bouquet. From the beginning, David had showered her with flowers which had dutifully arrived every Friday. They were beautiful expensive bouquets lovingly arranged by an expert florist, but other than paying for them he had never done anything as important as choosing them himself. In fact she suspected one of the junior clerks had been assigned the task and no doubt when they had moved up to Yorkshire he would have switched the weekly order to a delighted local florist.

The carelessly wrapped bunch of blue flowers Gareth handed over meant a lot to her and she took them from him, kissing him on the cheek.

'Thanks. They're lovely.'

'You've been away.'

'So have you.'

'I tried to ring you. Do you always switch your mobile off?'

'Quite often. What do you think?' she asked quickly before he had time to ask about her time up north, distracting him by whirling round to indicate the newly decorated hall.

'It looks fabulous. Different,' he said. 'No carpet.'

'You'd better like these tiles. I spent ages cleaning them.'

'They are lovely. You've got rid of the flowery wallpaper too I see.'

'Well yes, it was overkill, don't you think?' She was pleased with the reaction and knew that he liked it. 'Have you heard from Pamela and Richard at all?'

'I've had a postcard. They seem to be settling in nicely. She asked after you.'

'That was nice of her.' She smiled at him. 'Come on through to the kitchen. Most of my budget disappeared on that.'

She was terribly proud of it, keen to show it off to Selina when she finally made it down here. She wasn't quite as gadget conscious as Selina and she did wonder as she stacked her collection of cookery books on a shelf whether she would ever get the chance to entertain again. Sitting eating here in the kitchen would not have met with David's approval, but David was no longer here, she reminded herself, and she was getting used to solitary meals again.

'Wow.' Gareth duly admired it. 'Very nice. You have been busy.'

He wandered round, examining things as she found a jug for the flowers and got the mugs out for the coffee. Only now did she notice that he seemed ill at ease, marking time, something on his mind, and she hoped she was not in for another confession. Just now, she could not cope with that.

'Come and sit down. I've got something to tell you,' he said.

'Oh.' Her heart sank. 'If it's about the accident you had, Gareth, you have to put it out of your mind. It was not your fault. Forget it, please. You're making much too much of it.'

'No, it's not that. In fact, I think talking to you helped me. You're right. I've been brooding about it for far too long. No wonder they all got fed up with me at the office. I did blow it up out of all proportion and I am doing what you say and trying to put it out of my mind. It was not my fault. Accidents happen but it's taken a long time for me to accept that.'

'Thank heavens for that.' She smiled. 'How was London?'

'All right. It's funny how quickly you forget how crowded it is. I was glad to get back.'

'I miss it sometimes,' she confessed. 'I don't miss the crowds, but I do miss little things.'

'You can always visit.'

'Oh yes and I intend to. Where did you stay?'

'At one of the modern chains. Nowhere special.'

'What were you up to or is it a secret?'

'It's no secret. I was speaking at a seminar.'

'Were you now?' she teased. 'You do like to hide your light under a bushel. It sounds very important.'

'Not a bit of it. It was just a small gathering,' he said quickly. 'There were thirty or so people there. I'm on a speaker list so I get called on from time to time. They were mostly new business graduates, all very keen. It was a pleasure to talk to them. The worrying thing is it's all moving very fast, Francesca, and it won't be long before I'm hopelessly out of touch. I'll have to bow out shortly before they kick me off the list.'

'Why did you give up your job, Gareth? Was it after the accident?'

'Not too long after. I was OK at first, shocked but all right. But then when news got around, when it was in the papers, everybody was so sympathetic it started to get to me. It was very difficult hearing all about her at the inquest, about what a talented girl she had been, about her hopes and ambitions. It brought her to life for me.'

'There must have been witnesses, people who saw what happened?'

'Oh yes. Her father came over afterwards, shook my hand, told me it wasn't my fault, but her mother couldn't look me in the eye.'

'That's mothers for you,' she said quietly, thinking of her own.

'It killed my relationship with my girlfriend. Helen ...' he grimaced. 'She was sympathetic at first but after a while she started to harp on at me to pull myself together, but it wasn't as simple as that. I couldn't get that vision out of my head because straight after the accident I stumbled across to the car and saw her slumped and bleeding you see. I think I knew straightaway she wasn't going to survive.'

'Oh Gareth.'

He looked up and tried a smile. 'It wasn't Helen's fault but she couldn't cope with me like that. On top of that it was affecting my work and I didn't want to do it any more. I quit without discussing it with her and she really blew her top at that and soon after that we split up.'

'Do you regret it?' Francesca asked, holding her breath.

'Splitting up? Or quitting the job?'

'Both.'

'I don't regret either. The job was no longer what it was and it wasn't working with Helen. We both knew that. It was just a matter of time.'

'I used to work in advertising,' she said. 'It was about as stressful as it gets, but at one time I used to thrive on it. It was never boring. I was on the creative team and I'll never forget the horror of doing a presentation to prospective clients. Awful heart stopping moments just before you go into the room but exhilarating for all that especially if you knew you had a great idea.'

'It sounds as if you enjoyed it?'

'Yes. And I was good at it, Gareth. David was not keen on my continuing to work after we got married and we were moving to Yorkshire anyway so I had to resign but the truth is ...' she hesitated because she was going to criticize her late husband. 'I had started looking for jobs in that area without telling him. There was no way I was going to go on the ladies who lunch circuit even if that's what he expected of me.'

'That might have been tricky for you.'

'Yes. It would have been an uphill struggle.'

There was a moment's silence, but she did not want to discuss David further and he seemed to sense that.

'Anyway, back to the seminar,' he said. 'Guess who I met there?'

'I have no idea,' she said.

'Clive Foster.'

'Selina's Clive?'

'Yes. We knew each other vaguely from way back. We were once in the same company believe it or not, but in different departments so we were never close but I remembered him straightaway. At six-five he makes a big impression, a larger than life character. Not someone you forget in a hurry.'

'How did you make the connection with me?'

'It came out as we chatted and I said I had moved to the West Country. He asked if I knew you.' He smiled. 'I think he imagined that just because I knew Devon I might know you. And, as it turned out, coincidence won.'

'I might have mentioned you when I last spoke to Selina,' Francesca said feeling a little nervous now for she didn't like the thought of the two men talking about her behind her back. 'She wanted to know all about the people I'd met down here and she has a habit of getting every last scrap of information out of me. Did you meet her too?'

'As a matter of fact I did. Wives are not normally at these dos but they had an informal get-together later at the hotel and yes I met her. In fact when she found out who I was she cornered me and said she wanted a word.'

'What did she want to talk to you about?' Francesca pushed his tea at him and some biscuits. She felt awkward suddenly for he was awkward, too, and she hoped that Selina had not been sticking her oar in, extolling her virtues and so on.

Selina should learn to mind her own business.

Whilst Francesca liked and was attracted to Gareth and there was no point in denying it, she was a long way off a deep commitment. Despite everything, despite the doubts that had started up, she still felt married to David, was still dreaming about him and it was unforgivable of Selina to think that there was an easy fix. A quick shag even with somebody as nice as Gareth was not going to do it for her and next time, if there was a next time, she would be a lot more cautious before diving headlong into a relationship.

'You can tell me,' she went on quietly as Gareth seemed reluctant to proceed. 'What has she been saying? Whatever it is you can take it with a pinch of salt.'

'Oh Francesca, I don't like to do this. I'm not even sure if I should be doing it. I debated on the way over whether I should just forget it and keep you in the dark.'

'For God's sake,' she spluttered, feeling a vice tighten round her chest. 'Gareth, you drive me mad sometimes. Just spit it out. What on earth is it?'

'OK. She wanted to warn me off. She said some nasty things about you. She called you a conniving bitch if you must know. I don't believe a word of it, but I have to say with friends like that who needs enemies?'

'She called me what?' Francesca might have been in space

for she truly felt gravity pushing her down into the chair, her body a dead weight. 'Is this a joke?' she managed to say at last even though she knew it was not.

'Sorry.'

The betrayal was so colossal that she could say nothing more. Seeing her face, Gareth rose quickly to his feet, raised her off the chair and gathered her into his arms, holding her close and stroking her hair.

'Hey, it's not as bad as that. If it's any consolation she's just the type of woman I despise. She's cold and calculating and on the surface bloody successful at what she does, but who knows what goes on behind the scenes. Has it occurred to you that she might be jealous?'

'I can't think why.' Francesca sniffed. She was being daft, behaving like a little girl losing her best friend, but why should it be any different just because you were grown-up? 'She's got so much. She has Clive and the children and a fantastic career. What more could she want? And, look at me, what have I got? Money, yes, but I don't have anybody, Gareth. I lost David and sometimes that's hard to bear.'

'You've got *me*,' he whispered. 'I know I can't compare to your husband, but I'm here whenever you're ready.'

She made no attempt to wriggle free. It was a relief to be held tight by a man and just at that moment she savoured it.

Bit by bit it came out over another cup of tea.

Francesca wanted to know everything Selina had said and how she had looked as she said it. She even wanted to know what she was wearing at the time as if that had any bearing whatsoever on what had happened.

The red dress. A gorgeous designer one if Francesca was remembering it. Well, that figured, she supposed, for it fitted

Selina like a glove showing off her enviable and, after three children, surprisingly toned shape but somehow the colour was not so good on a blonde and she could see very clearly the pale ethereal face and the brightness of the blue eyes as Gareth tried stumblingly to describe it and her.

The poor guy was as confused and angry as she was. He barely knew Selina and Clive nor did he know Francesca that well but he was firmly on her side. He hadn't been taken in by those baby blue eyes and he didn't know what on earth she was playing at but, whatever it was, he didn't like it. From what he said she gathered that Selina was livid as the cruel words escaped her lips although fortunately she kept her voice low to avoid a scene.

'Why did she tell you?' Francesca asked at last.

'I was around and you weren't. Who's to know what her motive was? Maybe she'd had a few too many Martinis,' he said. 'Although that's no excuse.'

'You'd better go, I think,' she told Gareth, still reeling both from the shock of what he had said and from the way she felt as he held her. She had wanted him to kiss her but he had not or rather he had merely dropped a kiss on top of her head.

She knew he wanted her at that moment and he was behaving in a very gentlemanly fashion which both pleased and irritated her. She was mixed up emotionally and needed time on her own to think about things. She was missing not so much the sex but the need to be held close by somebody stronger than her, physically stronger anyway. It was a normal reaction, why a toddler reaches up to adults, a need to feel safe and protected.

It was more than that, though. It felt perilously special when Gareth held her, his stubble a little rough against her cheek, smelling of soap and a nice aftershave. As he held her, she knew that it would have taken so little, emotionally shot as she was at that moment, to drag him upstairs to her bed to offer some comfort.

But she had resisted and let him go instead.

Chapter Sixteen

WHEN HE WAS gone, she arranged the flowers in the jug, placing it on the wide window sill of the sitting-room, standing there and looking out onto rain. Today the rain seemed indecisive, alternating between stair-rods and light drizzle and as she opened the window and leaned out the smell was fresh, the garden soaking up the much needed moisture from days of relentless sun.

Good.

The river was low and they needed a deluge like this, several of them, to reduce the threat of a hosepipe ban. Closing the window, she busied herself for a while with routine chores, none of which really needed doing, but it seemed a good way to keep her feelings under control by concentrating on the normal every-day things, things she could do on automatic domestic pilot.

The problem was the words 'conniving bitch' kept spinning around in her head and at the last she relented, made herself a drink and plonked down on the sofa, thinking back to the first time she met Selina as if somehow that might help her to understand why she had turned against her in the way she had.

Francesca's life had been simple in the days before David had appeared and become part of her routine, or rut, whichever way you chose to look at it. She had a modest pleasant enough one-bedroom flat on the first floor with cheery blinds at the windows to avoid looking out onto a not very inspiring view of the city. It was in a handy position not far from the tube station and, having climbed onto that difficult first rung of the property ladder she was in no hurry to move on.

She hoped for something bigger and better one day, but made the best of it. She was paid a reasonable salary and she only had herself to look after. Her social life, however, could only be described as dull and, as she grew older, it became trickier. She was at that funny in-between stage, too old for the after-student life and too young to take up with some of the older ladies in her apartment block who had made friendly overtures inviting her to go to concerts and so on. She regretted turning them down once too often and eventually, not surprisingly, they had stopped asking.

Francesca did not often join her work colleagues for an evening drink, but the day she met Selina she had been persuaded to even though she worried that she did not quite fit into their little circle; she was older than most of them even if she was not quite old enough to be their mother, but it felt very much like that as she listened, smiling determinedly to show she was not shocked at their sometimes outrageous conversation.

They were an outgoing lot, smart and savvy – a necessary trait in the world in which they worked – and in a way it was she, quieter and more solitary who was a little at odds with her profession. She might not be as pushy or edgy as they were, but she was the one who came up with the ideas as often as not and that was why they looked up to her and why she earned three times as much as they did. Their chat was trivial, funny and often they talked with fond exasperation about their mothers and fathers, just the sort of chat she could not participate in for fear of bringing the whole cheerful session to a grinding and awkward halt.

A casually dropped remark; I very nearly killed my only brother and my mother hated me and she's dead and I haven't a clue where my father is because he walked out on us when I was ten would cause a horrified silence followed quickly by a wave of sympathy and maybe an understanding at last of why she, Francesca Blackwell, was a nice enough woman in their eyes but of a complicated frame of mind and ever so slightly distant.

They had become a trifle insistent though, and eventually they wore her down so, in order to stop their innocent questioning, one day out of the blue she invented a nice sounding mum and dad who lived in the country and had two lively spaniel dogs and a big garden. Why the spaniels she had absolutely no idea and it was dangerous to embark on large-scale deception because a casual remark would be remembered. One girl, an animal lover, had immediately brightened when the dogs were mentioned asking what their names were.

She would never do this again, Francesca vowed, coming up with plausible sounding doggy names and wishing the floor would swallow her up. Thereafter she confined the loving mum and dad and the dogs to obscurity before she expanded on them and it became a total nonsense. In the event it caused a minor problem at David's funeral somebody asked if her parents were here and for a moment, stunned as she was, she could only shake her head and worry herself sick during the opening hymn that the absence of her fictitious parents might get back to Selina.

Sitting among her colleagues on the occasions she did have a drink with them, she spent the time listening much more than offering a contribution to the conversation, and was reminded of similar one-sided conversations with Izzy. It seemed she was destined to be the listener, forever the shy one sitting on the sidelines and, as with Izzy of old, some of the tales she was listening to were indeed gloriously indiscreet. Francesca took her job seriously, working her socks off when in the office and, cocooned as she was in her particular slot there, the various romantic escapades that were taking place right in front of her completely passed her by.

'I could swear they'd been at it, there and then, just minutes before,' one of the girls was saying, finishing off her piece of juicy gossip. 'You only had to look at her. And him.'

They took a delighted moment to absorb this and Francesca knew with some regret that she would never be able to look that particular man in the face again without conjuring up a picture of him and his secretary enjoying a private moment in his office. It was incredible and his wife whom she had met once seemed such a nice woman.

'What's happening in your love life, Francesca?' somebody asked.

'Nothing much.'

She saw the looks the younger girls exchanged, momentarily irritated that they might be under the impression that she had never had sex in her life and thus provoked she felt she ought to enlighten them and for once give as good as she got. If she stuck to facts instead of lying it would be all right.

'I've had my moments. I was with somebody for two years, somebody I met at university,' she said. 'He was a doctor called Andrew and he wanted us to get married.'

'But you didn't?'

Well, obviously not.

She saw the questioning look in their eyes and felt compelled to elaborate on it, exaggerate it in fact by making him out to be film-star handsome aware that they placed great store in how people looked. It was the job of course, all about presentation. Did she have a photo? No she did not. Why on earth would she carry a photograph of a man she was long over.

In fact Andrew had been Mr Ordinary, nothing to write home about so far as looks went and none of these girls would have given him a second glance. There was more to life than that though. He was charming and thoughtful and they had a lot in common and talking about it was making her feel sad.

'Who dumped who?' one of the girls asked and the others smiled and looked at her kindly and she knew that they thought she was making it all up which was ridiculous because this time it happened to be true.

'It was a mutual decision,' Francesca said, wishing she hadn't got started on it now. 'He wanted us to get married and he became very broody. He started talking about the children we would have one day and I had to be honest with him. I don't want children. I've never wanted children and I shall never have children.'

'Quite right too,' a voice said and there was Selena being swooped on by one of their party. She was wearing a well cut navy work-suit and a plain cream silk blouse and ordered a large gin and tonic before inserting herself between them at the table, expensive rings glinting, perfectly groomed at that. Within minutes of arriving, her drink in hand, she took charge of the conversation.

'I think you're very brave,' she said, beaming at Francesca. 'You must never have children just because it's what everybody expects and never be fooled by all those gorgeous babies in those adverts.'

They laughed at that. That was what they did, subtly direct-ing people towards a particular product with no qualms about how they might achieve that.

'Believe me and I speak from experience, once you have a baby, you are completely—' she lowered her voice before telling them causing another round of laughter. She exchanged a knowing glance with Francesca, a woman of her own age and for a moment they shared the feeling of being older and infi-nitely wiser.

By the end of the little session, Selina had taken Francesca under her wing telling her that she knew this marvellous man and would she like her to arrange an introduction? He didn't want children either so there would be no problems with that.

'No, absolutely not.' Francesca said firmly, astonished at the audacity of the woman whom she had only just met. Selina soothed her by saying that it was nothing like a blind date, that it would not be as obvious as that and that it was entirely up to Francesca how it progressed after the introduction.

'It's just a little fun,' she said.

And so, egged on by the others, deciding that her life was a little short on adventure, she accepted the invitation to join the lady at some fancy law society dinner.

'It's impossible to be over-dressed on these occasions,' Selina warned her. 'The wives keep dragging out these ball-gowns year after year so do go for something extravagant. Something frilly and low cut.'

It was a good excuse for a new frock and she chose an expen-sive chocolate brown strapless number nipped in at the waist with a full swishy skirt and discreet jewellery. As Selina's guest, her husband being unavailable, she felt overcome by a girlish shyness as she followed Selina who, dressed in a burnt orange off-the-shoulder dress with a huge bow, powered ahead of her into the room.

'Now where the hell has he got to?' Selina said when she caught up. 'Don't worry. It won't be the least obvious. He's a darling man and he needs a woman.'

'Does he know that?' Francesca asked with a smile.

'He's been on the look-out for ages, but he can't find his Miss Right, bless him. Oh, did I mention that he's quite a bit older than us. He's a very young sixty something,' she said, smiling as she caught Francesca's consternation.

Oh dear God. She very nearly beat a hasty retreat there and then, would have but Selina was holding onto her arm as if she was one of her children trying to wriggle free. The grip was firm but friendly and, short of making a scene, she had no option but to go through with it.

So, she recalled, it was all down to Selina's pushiness that she had met David in the first place but now she seemed to be saying that Francesca had married him for his money and the prestige which was quite wrong although, she could not deny that, following his death, she had, to put it crudely, copped the lot.

According to Gareth, Selina had been expecting David's paintings to go to her and was furious that Francesca had sold them. But why hadn't she said as much? And David had certainly never said as much either but if she was going to kick up such a fuss she could have had the damned things. Francesca remembered that she had wanted to know which of David's two favourite charities would be benefiting from the sale of the paintings and Francesca had told her. Now it seemed that Selina, using her many connections, had had the gall to check up on that, discovering no doubt that neither of them had in fact received substantial donations from her, not yet.

She was livid both at Selina and whoever at the charity had divulged the information but it was done now and there was little point in pursuing that further.

Francesca did not have to explain herself. She was not depriving his charities in any way and would make sure that they did each receive a large sum. Just now, with much juggling of funds involved, she had pinpointed what she had earned from the sale of the paintings to her own good cause, and if David was here, he would understand.

The anger abated and in its place there were tears. How dare Selina, sitting in her own smug, snug little world, make judgements about her and her motives when really she knew nothing about her?

She wished now she had made an effort to get in touch with Izzy. There was no need to put on an act with Izzy because she understood what was what. She should have told her that David had died because, notwithstanding Gareth's sturdy offering she also needed a womanly shoulder to cry on.

They alone, she and Izzy, shared a secret that they had kept from her mother for years.

They alone knew what had really happened that day.

As a result of Francesca's incompetence, her brother James was permanently brain damaged.

And had been for the last twenty-six years.

Chapter Seventeen

AFTER AN UNCOMFORTABLE night full of disturbed dreams, her first thought next day was to ring Selina and have it out with her.

But even as she lifted the receiver and dialled her home number it occurred that Selina would be in the office by now with her secretary fielding her calls so she hung up. It had not been the best of ideas anyway because it was impossible to have a good old head to head argument on the telephone and one or other of them would only end up slamming down the receiver or worse in tears. The alternative was a terse text message but that seemed silly and inappropriate and she had too much to say anyway.

Should she contact Clive and ask him what the hell his wife was playing at? He was an affable steady guy and she felt she could talk to him for he might be able to throw some light on it although the last thing she wanted was to throw a spoke in the wheel of his apparently blissfully happy marriage to Selina. Contacting him would be too sneaky a thing to do and she discounted that almost as soon as she thought it.

David would be shocked and appalled.

He had liked Selina even though in private he was often scathing about her and about the way she lived her life.

She recalled those cheery dinner parties in the kitchen at

Selina's where David appeared to relax, happy for Selina to tease him and giving as good as he got. He liked Selina because she was in no way in awe of him and he accepted her gentle teasing not to mention a little flirting in good part. He liked Clive, too, so far as she knew although they were a little far removed in age to be drinking buddies.

Feeling upset by the accusation Selina had thrown at her was giving her the excuse for self-pitying thoughts and she was not going to give Selina the satisfaction of letting any of this bother her.

On second thoughts, she would sit tight.

She was not going to make any move she might regret and it would be up to Selina whether or not *she* did. Having decided that, she felt a bit better and because sitting cooped up in the house was doing her no good at all she went out.

It was still cloudy and spitting with rain as she hastened down the path, clicking open the gate and looking back at the house she knew so well and, as she always did, she half expected to see her mother standing there in the porch, smiling and waving her off, holding onto James's hand. She had been jealous of the time the two of them spent together when she was at school, doing things she was excluded from and, although she did try to play with him when he was little, he pushed her aside as often as not. He liked rough and tumble games, not interested in jigsaws and story books. Sometimes she thought it would all have been so different if he had been a girl; a little sister was something she could have coped with so much better.

Her mother might be gone, but her presence lingered in the house, in odd corners, and vulnerable as she was just now, Francesca imagined a shadow flitted around sometimes at the extreme edge of her peripheral vision – gone of course the minute she turned to confront it. Sometimes too she would snatch a sniff of perfume in the room that had been her parents' bedroom, instantly recognisable as the one used by her mother.

More than anything, after the accident, she had craved forgiveness but her mother had failed to provide it. More than anything, she had wanted her mother to scoop her up in her arms and tell her that it wasn't her fault, but that had never happened.

She and Izzy did not know on the day that James nearly drowned that a walker was heading their way, coming down the steep rocky path that led from the moor. He did not witness exactly what happened, hearing the commotion and setting himself the task of getting down the tricky terrain in one piece. He was not a young man, but as soon as he got there, having ascertained that Izzy knew what she was doing in administering first aid, he raced to the house by the river to raise the alarm.

Things escalated then and by the time he arrived back with the lady of the house in tow, an ambulance was already on its way and James was breathing again thanks to Izzy's determined efforts. Standing uselessly by her side, Francesca had watched Izzy coming into her own, no longer the flirty carefree person she liked to present to the world but a competent unflappable girl, somebody who knew exactly what she was doing. With her hair plastered to her face and her clothes clinging damply to her, rivulets of water streaming down her face, she ignored all thoughts of herself, her concentration centred on what her hands were doing to his limp little body.

'For heaven's sake, Izzy.' She heard herself speak as the

seconds ticked by and there was no response. After what seemed forever, she almost said 'he's dead, leave it', but even as she struggled to say the words he moved.

James breathed again thanks to Izzy, coughing and spluttering and bringing up a good lungful of water and gunge, but since then he had not really come round, not properly, and his general floppiness and state of stupor was enough to cause panic.

Shocked and confused, all Francesca could think about as the lady of the house dried her and Izzy off was that moment when she opened her eyes, raised her body up to rest on her elbows and saw him standing there balanced on the parapet. Wrapped, still shivering, in a blanket, she could remember that the shock of it had rendered her completely helpless, immobile and speechless, and, as if in a nightmare, she could not do anything, say anything, eyes fixed on him as he did his wobbly tightrope walk, until beside her Izzy stirred, sat up abruptly and saw what was happening and, without a second's grace immediately screamed at him.

'Get down this minute, you silly little sod.'

She shouldn't have done that.

The act of half turning was enough to upset his balance and with a yell he slipped and fell then in the worst possible position almost at the centre of the bridge. The splash was restrained with no spluttering and waving of arms, no re-emerging and then going under again. The water, at its darkest, deepest and most sinister, simply closed over him, the river shelving deeply in the centre. He could probably have made an attempt to swim but he was wearing his clothes and sandals and that made it so different from the splashing about he enjoyed in the pale chlorinated blue of the leisure pool.

'Bloody hell, Francesca, do something,' Izzy said, already whipping off her skirt to reveal her knickers, kicking off her shoes, preparing to go in even though it was Francesca who was by far the stronger swimmer. She, however, was rooted to the spot.

With no thought for her own safety, Izzy was in the water in a flash, wading in until the bottom slipped away from her and then swimming with very ungainly splashy strokes, reaching the spot somehow where James had last been seen. Taking a deep breath, she then submerged herself.

'Oh God, oh God …' Francesca was wailing now, fearing that, unless she did something they might both drown. Izzy popped up, gasping for air, before going down again and then, galvanised into action at last, Francesca set off, slip-sliding as her feet moved against the muddy bottom of the shallows, catching hold of James just as Izzy surfaced with him, grabbing him off her and leaving Izzy to make her own ungainly way back to the river's edge.

'You were a fat lot of use,' Izzy said as she struggled out, her blouse sticking to her body, slime and mud coating her bottom half. 'Did you want the little beggar to drown? Give him to me.' Feet squelching in the mud, she pushed Francesca aside then and started the business of helping the limp little body that was James. She had done a resuscitation course and was finally given the opportunity of putting it into practice.

There followed a fiasco of immense proportions with the ambulance getting stuck in the lane but the crew were brilliant when they did arrive and by the time they got to the hospital, Francesca was breathing a sigh of relief, confident that, once the doctors and nurses got their hands on him, all would be well.

But it was not as simple as that.

James had been under water a while and whilst some children would probably recover more or less unharmed after suffering short term submersion – a near drowning – some would die and some would be left with moderate neurological problems from which they might be expected to get better. All this was very positive but there was a slim chance it could result in more permanent brain damage if, during the submersion, James had picked up waterborne bacteria for instance.

They found out about all that later. They had technical terms for it and explanations but it made no difference. Call it what you will, when you got down to it, James was just one of the unlucky ones.

'She'll kill me,' Francesca said as they waited at the hospital for her mother to arrive, unaware at that time of course of the extent of the damage. 'It's all my fault. I promised her I wouldn't go near the river. If he dies, she'll kill me.'

'He's not going to die,' Izzy said calmly, putting her arm round her.

'Look at you. Your blouse is ruined.'

'It's just a cheap thing from Dorothy Perkins,' Izzy said, catching her glance. 'What does it matter?'

'I know. I'm being daft.'

'Don't you dare go hysterical on me,' Izzy told her, watching her closely. 'It's going to be all right. He started breathing again, didn't he? And it is not your fault. It's his for being so stupid. I distinctly remember you telling him not to climb onto the bridge.'

Francesca gave her a look. Nice try, Izzy, but she had said no such thing.

'We can't blame him,' she said. 'He's just a little boy. I can swim better than you. If I'd dived in straightaway I would have got him out sooner.'

'Well, you didn't, did you and we can do sod all about that

now. I'm trying to help you here, Francesca. I'll say it was my idea to go down to the river so that I could have a smoke.'

'No.' Francesca drew a sharp breath. 'Don't mention smoking. She doesn't know I smoke.'

'It's just an excuse,' Izzy said, voice low. 'We have to get the story straight. I'll say it was all my idea if it helps get you off the hook. We won't tell her you froze. You couldn't help it. I've heard about that happening to people. People stuck on a mountain ledge who suddenly can't move a muscle. That's what happened to you.'

Froze? Yes that was exactly what had happened, but not before the awful thought had flashed through her head that, if James was gone, it could all go back to the way it had been before he arrived. Her mother might have some time for her again. Had that very thought stopped her from doing anything? She could not bear to think of it now for, if it had, then that very nearly made her a murderer or she would have been if he had drowned.

'Best not tell your mum what happened,' Izzy said. 'We'll say it was you who dived in and got him out. That sounds better. It was you who dived in and untied him ...'

'Untied him?'

'Even though it was murky, I saw him straightaway but he was tangled up in weeds,' Izzy told her with a shudder. 'I've no idea what they were but they were wrapped round him and he had struggled and made it worse. Look ...' she showed her hands which had scratches on them. 'I tell you I thought I wasn't going to make it. Another minute and I would have had to come up without him. I was bursting to breathe.'

'Thanks, Izzy. You were fantastic.'

'Not really. We couldn't just stand around and let him drown, could we?'

'I'm his sister not you,' Francesca said sharply. 'If I'd jumped in before you, I would have got him out quicker than you, wouldn't I? You can't even swim properly. I'd have got there in half the time it took you,' she finished bitterly, knowing she was not making sense, knowing that it was terrible of her to take it out on Izzy.

'You've already said all that so shut up now. Just look at us. Look at my hair.' She pulled at it, frizzing up as it was. 'My mum's going to go spare. That was a new blouse, cheap or not.'

'I'll buy you another.'

'No you won't. Sorry.' Izzy sighed, putting an arm round her. 'It doesn't matter. All that matters is that we got him out and got him breathing again.'

'She's here.' Francesca stiffened in Izzy's arms.

Izzy looked up as Francesca's mother walking very quickly headed down the corridor, hair awry, her face dreadful to behold. 'Let me do the talking. You'll only put your foot in it.'

And so it was Izzy who came up with the lie and she did nothing to stop it.

Whether or not her mother believed her was another matter, but it was Izzy who covered for her, Izzy who took the blame. It had been Izzy's idea to go down to the river so that she could indulge in a spot of smoking and James had climbed onto the parapet even though Francesca had told him not to.

Worse, she went on to say how it was Francesca who had jumped in without a moment's hesitation and pulled him out. Even worse, the local paper got wind of it and published a little article where they hailed her as a heroine, "Sister saves little brother".

Her mother took it all in, listening to Izzy, but looking only at Francesca and it was soon after that, when they understood the extent of the harm that had come to him that the icy veil came down between them, a veil that was never ever lifted.

When they were able to bring him home, just a shadow of the James that once was, she stood helplessly by as her mother gently lifted him from his wheelchair and settled him in the chair in the sitting-room, lifting up his legs for him and putting them on the footstool, tucking a blanket round him, stroking his face and fussing him as if he were a baby again.

Her eyes met Francesca's as she stood up and it was like looking at a stranger, a stranger who despised her.

'Are you satisfied now, madam?' she said softly. 'Just look what you've done.'

Thinking about James and her mother was a mistake and, to make her feel better, Francesca popped into her favourite café for a coffee and a slice of apple cake with a dab of clotted cream. She picked up a newspaper from the rack and found herself a corner table where she could watch the comings and goings. It was mid afternoon and lunch was over so it was fairly quiet. Opening up the paper, Francesca almost hid behind it, not wanting conversation today.

Conniving bitch. The words echoed in her head. What had happened to make Selina hate her so?

The door jangled open and a woman and a girl came in standing with their backs to Francesca. The woman was wearing tight white cropped trousers, not a good choice for a big bottomed lady, with Cleopatra-type gold sandals, a disastrous choice for a day like today. Her hair, dark with a reddish tint, was up in a bouncy ponytail. Idly, Francesca watched as the girl, her hair shorter and darker, turned, caught her eye and smiled at her as her mother read the specials board.

Francesca felt her heart tug.

There was something familiar about the girl.

And then, as the woman turned too, Francesca saw why.

It was Izzy and her daughter.

Chapter Eighteen

'WHAT ARE YOU doing here?' They spoke simultaneously, laughing and hugging as the girl looked bemusedly on.

'Your hair's different,' Izzy said when they finally surfaced.

Francesca laughed. 'Well, it is over twenty years since I last saw you.'

'Never! Is it really?' She turned to her daughter. 'Vicky, this is my best friend Francesca. We were at school together.'

Vicky smiled politely, so like her mother at that age that Francesca was quite startled by the resemblance.

Best friend? What a lovely idea and how very true it was. Despite the gap since they had last seen each other, Francesca felt immediately at home and comfortable with Izzy as the realisation hit home that she was just the same person as she had been all those years ago.

'How have we let all this time go by?' Izzy said. 'We kept saying we must meet up and we never did. Is that my fault or yours?'

'Both of our's I think. Come and sit down.'

They did so and the girl at the counter cast them a glance but left them to it.

'Francesca Blackwell …' Izzy grinned at her. 'You couldn't wait to get away, could you? When you went away to university I never thought that would be the last time I would see you.'

'I would have come back during the holidays,' Francesca said apologetically. 'I meant to but Mother moved to Kent and that was that.'

'Oh yes. I remember the house going up for sale. She never told anybody where she was going. I'm sorry but my mum could never get on with her.' She smiled a rueful smile. 'You look different, Francesca, and it's not just the hair. You're very smart. Francesca works in advertising in London, Vicky.'

'Do you?' Vicky looked at her as if she was from another planet. 'Do you honestly? That's wicked. I want to live in London one day. I'm going to work in fashion.'

'You and a thousand others, Sweetheart.' Izzy softened the disparaging remark by smiling at her daughter and then looking at Francesca. 'Thanks for the birthday card by the way although I'm not sure I like to be reminded I'm another year older.'

'That's all right.' Francesca hesitated but Izzy beat her to it.

'Come on then, where is he hiding? This new husband of yours? I'm dying to meet him.'

Francesca gave an imperceptible shake of her head, glancing at the girl and Izzy, ever quick to sense a hesitation, picked up on it at once.

Time to get rid of Vicky.

'Look, Darling …' she rifled in her bag and produced a purse, handing a note to her daughter who had been standing quietly like a gooseberry for the last few minutes shaking her head though in a rather maternal way at their girlish excitement. 'Here's a tenner. Why don't you have a wander round town, get yourself something, whilst I have a chat with Francesca. I won't be long. You can text me if you need me.'

'OK.' Vicky pocketed the money. 'Thanks, Mum. Meet you back at the car in an hour?'

'Fine.'

Vicky sauntered off and Izzy watched her go.

'Isn't she lovely?'

'She looks just like you, Izzy.'

'She's not as crazy as I was. She's going to do well in her exams and she's quite determined to go to Art College. Knowing her, she'll get there too.'

After a few minutes, they left the café, Izzy doing most of the chatting as usual. She hadn't changed much apart from putting on weight, but that had always been on the cards with her. In any case although Francesca wouldn't dream of saying it, it suited her.

'Now, for heavens sake, out with it, what are you doing here? Is it a trip down memory lane? That's what we're up to. This place never changes, does it? I just dragged Vicky down to the canal to see our old house. That was a mistake I can tell you. It made me feel all weepy and I just kept looking at it until Vicky said somebody was watching us through the window and it looked like we were stalking them.' She smiled a little. 'I had a happy childhood, Francesca. I have lots of happy memories.'

'I know. You were so lucky, Izzy. How are your mum and dad these days?'

'Fine. They retired to Torquay. They have a little flat near the sea and we see a lot of them. It's good for the kids to see them. Mum spoils them something rotten.' She regarded Francesca with suspicious eyes. 'What's all this about then? Didn't it work out? Is it over? Have you left him?'

'He died, Izzy.'

'Oh my God, he didn't?'

'Yes he did. I left him sitting in the chair and when I got back he was dead. No fuss. No nothing. But then he wasn't the sort to make a fuss, not even of dying.'

Izzy put a hand over her mouth. 'So soon? I don't know what to say. You poor love, come here.'

In the middle of the street, oblivious to people passing by, she hugged her as a mother would and the gesture was so Izzy, such a blessed comfort, that it was all Francesca could do to stop herself from crying.

'I know why you're here then,' she said, her voice muffled in Francesca's blouse. You've come back here to get yourself together, haven't you?'

'That was the idea I suppose, but the old house was up for sale and I ended up buying it.' She hesitated feeling an explanation was needed. 'We were in the process of moving and David left me comfortably off so at least financially I'm OK.'

'Let me get this straight. You've bought Lilac House?'

'Yes. I live there now. Why don't you come round to see it? Now if you like.'

'Could I? I'd love that.'

'Come on then. I'll make you that coffee you never got round to having.'

'Vicky seems a nice girl,' Francesca said, noticing that Izzy quietened as they neared the house. 'You're lucky.'

'I know I am. I have four girls and they're all different. I've left Alan looking after the others today so goodness knows what will have happened by the time I get back. But that's dads for you.' She looked uneasy suddenly, remembering. 'I don't suppose you've ever heard from your dad?'

'Well ...' she hesitated but within seconds she was blurting it all out, telling Izzy everything, about the way her mother forced him to resign from his job, about the birthday cards he sent that she never received, about the way he had forgiven her mother and even that James was not his child.

'He had no backbone,' Izzy said when she was finished. 'He should have fought his corner and told her where to get off.'

'He was a gentle man. He let people walk all over him. If only I'd known.'

'Poor Francesca. It always happens to you, doesn't it?'

'At least you got what *you* wanted. Your big happy family.'

Izzy cast a sharp glance her way and Francesca had to say swiftly that she had not intended it to sound sarcastic. She meant it.

'I can't pretend it's been easy,' Izzy said. 'It's been up and down. Alan runs his own painting and decorating business and I've been pregnant most of the time so it's not been easy for me to keep a full-time job. So, we've had a struggle with money but I wouldn't change it for the world.'

'Here we are.' Francesca unlatched the gate. 'Do you remember it?'

'I remember it,' she said softly.

They stood a moment, memories flooding back for both of them as they looked at the house that was the same yet in subtle ways different.

'It's hardly changed,' Izzy said with a sigh. 'I don't know how you can do it, Francesca. Looking at my old house made me feel … well, I don't know quite how it made me feel but I wouldn't like to live there again. I just couldn't. I've changed and I couldn't step back in time like this.'

Francesca quickly denied she was doing that, opening the door and shooing her inside where Izzy at once enthused about the interior, saying it was just like those houses you see in the magazines where there wasn't a thing out of place whereas, in her house, much as she tried, it always looked as if there'd been a whirlwind rushing through seconds earlier.

Proud and delighted at the compliment, Francesca opened

the door to the study where David's magnificent old desk took centre stage with some of his books on the shelves and one of the more traditional paintings she had kept on the wall. The room was never intended to be a shrine to him but in some ways it had become that even though Francesca did use this room and this desk.

Izzy went over to take a closer look at the painting.

It was by a northern artist, something picked up on his travels, a picture of his beloved Yorkshire dales close to where his and her father's ashes were now blown to the wind.

'I like this,' she said. 'He had good taste, your husband.'

That did it. Francesca caught her breath, stifling a sob, and Izzy, taking one look at her, put her arms round her, murmuring soothing words as if she was one of the children.

'It's all right. I'm fine. Give me a moment,' Francesca said, shaking her loose, accepting a tissue that Izzy produced from a pocket and stemming the tears. 'It's so annoying. It can just come over you at any time.'

'Don't worry about it. Is this him?' Izzy picked up a photograph on top of the desk. 'He looks ...'

'He was in his sixties, Izzy.' Francesca said, putting her out of her misery, sensing she was trying to find something nice to say about the man she had never met, a man who didn't take a particularly good photograph at that. She wanted to explain that actually he was much more handsome than the photograph suggested but what was the point. 'He was a good man,' she finished quietly watching as Izzy placed it reverently back in its place. 'He was difficult and self-opinionated and very awkward at times but ...'

'I know. They're all like that. Alan tried it on something rotten, but I've learnt how to deal with him. It's all about letting him think he has the upper hand.'

They stood a moment in front of his desk as if paying homage and then Izzy sighed and reached into her bag drawing out a tattered packet of cigarettes. 'There's just two left in it,' she told Francesca. 'They've been there for months. I suppose you could say they're my comfort blanket. If things get really bad I can still smoke them but I'm not going to. Do you still smoke?'

'No. But I've been tempted over these last few months.'

'Shall we?' Izzy dangled the packet in front of her. 'We could just smoke these two, one each. What do you think?'

Francesca laughed 'I think you never change, Izzy Burton.'

'Izzy Harrison,' she corrected with a smile. 'Just testing. I knew you'd say no and I'm sorry I ever got you started on them in the first place.'

Over coffee with the cigarettes confined to the bin, face to face at last, they gave each other a potted history of their lives over the past eighteen years, no holds barred.

'And you never heard from him again?' Izzy asked when Francesca had finished telling her about Andrew and the time after university when they lived together up in the Scottish borders. 'You just walked away? You gave up the chance of marrying a doctor? Were you mad?'

'It was one of those awful moments when it can go either way. I got the job in London without telling him I had even applied for it and when I broke the news he said that he'd get a job there too and we could find a place together, maybe push the boat out and go straightaway for the family home and I went daft at that point. He just didn't get it. He thought he would persuade me otherwise and that, sooner or later, I would cave in and have the babies he wanted.'

'Poor man. He must have loved you,' Izzy said gently. 'Do you know what happened to him?'

She shrugged. 'Not a clue. I did think a few years ago that it might be fun to try to find him but then I had second thoughts. He's bound to be married by now and it wouldn't be fair on him.'

'You've not forgotten him, have you?' Izzy pounced on that.

'Almost.' She smiled a little.

'You are a fool, Francesca. If he'd loved you enough then it wouldn't have mattered but you never gave him that chance, did you? It wouldn't have mattered to me and Alan. We are so looking forward to the day when there's just the two of us again.'

'You can say that,' she said a little bitterly. 'You're happy to be a walking baby-making machine. What would your Alan have said if you'd refused to have a baby?'

'I've just told you. It wouldn't have mattered. He was never fussed about having kids but I was determined. He wanted to stop at two but then we tried for a boy and then again.' She laughed. 'Then we drew the line. Four is enough for anybody.'

'You always said you'd have four children. Two of each.'

'Ah yes.' Izzy smiled. 'That didn't quite go according to plan not with four daughters but that doesn't matter.'

'Don't you regret that you never took up that offer of a university place?' Francesca hesitated. 'You could have got your degree, had a career and still have had time for your children.'

'Maybe but you know me, I didn't want to do it that way round,' Izzy said with that familiar stubborn tilt of her head. 'Why do we all have to conform and do what's expected of us? I've been happy helping Alan with the business but I have plans for the future.'

'Doing what?'

'Nursing.' Surprisingly she blushed. 'It's something I've always wanted to do and I'll start the course once Mabel goes to school.'

'You'll be good at it,' Francesca said remembering the calm and efficient way she had dealt with James. 'I hope it works out for you.'

'It will.' Izzy said, brimming with confidence. 'I make sure all my plans come about although obviously there are some things you can't plan for,' she added, giving Francesca a rueful smile and no doubt thinking about David.

'I have no idea what I'm going to do now,' Francesca said. 'I feel so lonely, Izzy.'

Izzy reached over, holding her hand a moment. 'Give yourself time,' she said. 'You'll meet somebody else. You're much too young to give up on men but don't rush into anything.'

'Anyway, what are you doing here apart from taking a trip down memory lane?' Francesca asked, changing the subject before it became too difficult. 'Are you still living in Kingsbridge?'

'Oh yes. We like it there. Alan's built up a good client base and he gets repeat jobs now but he hates taking time off. We could only afford to take a week's break and we didn't want to travel far so we're staying over in Cornwall at a cottage near Tintagel. Vicky thinks she's getting too old to come on holiday with us so we're making the most of it. This will be the last holiday I think that we're all together.'

A cottage in Tintagel? Ridiculously the coincidence was confirmed and Izzy beamed at her, stopping short of quizzing her about Gareth.

'Look, why don't we meet up later in the week? Come on over. I'd like you to meet Alan and he'll be thrilled to meet you. I've told him all about you.'

'Not everything surely?'

'You mean the James thing? No. I don't talk about that. I never told anybody, not even my mum.' Her expression changed to one of concern. 'How is he these days?'

'Not much change. He's not got a lot worse but they're aston-ished he's still with us. He got the use of his legs back although he gets tired quickly but he doesn't need the wheelchair all the time. You know what the prognosis was but he's got a strong heart and that keeps him going. It was hard for Mother but she would never accept help especially not from me but now that she's gone, he's had to go into a home where they can look after him. I know I should visit but I'm scared he won't know me. I was going to talk to David about it, ask him if he could come to live with us but I don't know if he would have agreed. There was no other option after Mother died,' she finished helplessly. 'Honestly, Izzy, how could I have looked after him, a single working woman? He needs constant care. He's a big man and I couldn't do it myself.'

'Bloody hell, Francesca, of course you couldn't. Can I say something awful?'

She nodded.

'I sometimes wonder if it wouldn't have been better if he hadn't survived. I brought him back from the dead, didn't I, but for what? So that he could be like that for the rest of his life.'

Before she left, they agreed to meet up at Tintagel where they would spend some time together even if it was only a lazy day pottering about. Francesca was keen to meet the other chil-dren and Alan too.

'You might regret it. It'll be chaotic,' Izzy warned. 'I know you're not keen on kids.'

'No, that's not true,' Francesca said wishing people could understand this. 'I love them, but I just don't want any of my own.'

'Right.' Izzy nodded and gave her a quick kiss. 'I have to

hand it to you, Francesca. I was wrong there. I thought you would change your mind.'

'You'd better get back to Vicky before she starts worrying where you are.'

'She's fine. If my mum taught me anything she taught me to give them a loose rein.'

Waving her off, Francesca had to recognize that, four children on, Izzy was looking rather ordinary. Of course cheap and cheerful holiday clothes, scraped back hair and very little make-up did not help, but she felt sad that the startlingly pretty Izzy of old had all but disappeared. Izzy had never been beautiful but she did have mischievous dark eyes and a knockout smile and had always been able to attract men.

If her eldest daughter Vicky was anything to go by Izzy had done a pretty good job of child rearing. Vicky seemed a sane and sensible girl at fifteen – unlike her mother at that age – and, just for a second, as she had watched the two of them together, almost physically aware of the mother/daughter bond that tied them, the one that she had never really shared with her own mother, she felt a pang.

Izzy, for better or worse had pretty much got what she wanted out of life.

Francesca was still searching.

Chapter Nineteen

WHAT TO DO for the best in Pamela's garden room provided Francesca with a few headaches. She ditched the out-dated festoon blinds opting for plain ones in a pale grey for a sun-trap like this could stand cooler shades. This would be her bolt-hole and she furnished it simply and sparsely, loving its wide windows that gave her such a wonderful view of the garden. It was now light and airy and she rated it as her favourite room in the whole house, one that she could use all year round.

She had re-engaged the gardener whom Pamela had employed; a taciturn man called Will who made up for his lack of chattiness by knowing all there was to know about his subject, advising her on what would be necessary to re-vamp the back garden so that it would be more like the garden she remembered. She helped out a bit, not wanting to get under his feet or up his nose come to that with her amateur messing about, but he did not mind and even gave her odd little jobs to do, simple tasks that did not stretch her too far.

He was out there now, sorting out a really overgrown area which she wanted to turn into a vegetable plot and Francesca was sitting in the garden-room, mulling over a business idea in her head, aware that, after buying the house on impulse, she had to take care not to dive into something else on a whim before she thought it through. Well on target with the house re-decoration, she was now bored and would have to do something to both occupy and stretch her before long.

The phone rang and she picked up the extension.

'I know, I know, you can shoot me later but please let me explain.' Selina's voice exploded into her ear. 'Please don't hang up. Look, I'm here in this God forsaken town of yours, in a car-park by the river and I'm absolutely whacked. I never knew it took so long to get here. How do I find you?'

Selina here? It took a minute to sink in.

'What makes you think I want to see you?'

'Oh come on, Francesca. Have a heart. Don't make me drive all the way back. I am also desperate for the loo and don't make me use public ones.'

'I'll walk down. I'll be there in five minutes.'

You had to hand it to her. When it came to an apology, Selina believed in the grand gesture. It would seem that she had left the children with Clive in Italy, flown home, collected the car and driven all the way to Devon to say sorry.

The flowers were exotic from an exclusive florists, a Mediterranean mix of sunny yellow and orange, but Francesca scarcely gave them a second glance, dumping them in the sink to deal with later. On seeing Selina in the car park, she had turned away from her hug, having the satisfaction of feeling the instant withdrawal. Well, what on earth could she expect?

On the short trip back to Lilac House, the tension in the air was almost palpable. Friends are acutely aware of such things and they were friends or had been once upon a time.

'I don't know what else I can do, darling, other than pros-trate myself at your feet and plead for forgiveness,' Selina began after she returned from visiting the downstairs cloakroom. They were sitting in Francesca's brand new kitchen, a kitchen that looked so unlike hers. There wasn't a peg board in sight, no well used cookery books with greasy, floury pages, no soft toys and definitely no sleeping cats.

But then, as Francesca ruefully admitted to herself, there was no heart to it. It looked like a showroom kitchen where they have tasteful displays of fruit – probably artificial for no apples could be that perfect – and just a few colourful bowls to tone and some shiny utensils. The oven was unused as yet, sparklingly clean.

Selina looked at her as she made no reply, pushing then at her hair, her beautifully cut hair that looked in need of a shampoo. She looked uncharacteristically rough, but Francesca could not drum up much sympathy. Silently she made coffee, instant with a slosh of milk from the carton. Sitting opposite the woman she thought of as her former friend, she could not be bothered with niceties, pushing biscuits across the table, still in their packet as if needing to emphasise their different priorities.

'No thank you,' Selina said, pushing them back. Her nail polish was chipped at that and, suddenly aware, she scrunched her fingers up and sighed. 'Look, I know it's no excuse, but I was half cut when I was talking to Gareth and I might have said things I didn't really mean. I shouldn't drink at all. It brings out the very worst in me. When I went over later what I had said I nearly died. Oh God ...' she said. 'Don't look like that. The truth is I haven't been strictly honest with you, darling. But I had my reasons. I know you loved David in your way,' she added with a knowing glance. 'And after he died it didn't seem fair to tell you.'

'Tell me what? Please get to the point.'

'Oh Lord, you are cross with me, aren't you?'

Francesca let out a sigh. The baby blue eyes were filling with tears but she hardened her heart. 'Conniving bitch!' How dare she and how dare she sit here in her kitchen trying to insinuate somehow that it was Francesca's fault. She had witnessed the way Selina sometimes dealt with her oldest son, the way she cleverly reasoned with him and got him to change his tune, the way she coaxed him into thinking he was in the wrong when very often he was not.

Well, that tactic would not work with *her*.

'I loved him. There were no doubts for me.' Selina said. 'I loved that bastard in a way that I shall never love Clive. David Porter was the love of my life. I think I loved him more than you did.'

Francesca started to protest but what was the use. Selina was perceptive if nothing else and had an unpleasant knack of being able to dig out the truth. She ought to have been the barrister, not David.

'Don't tell Clive I said that. Clive is very possessive.' she went on. 'The fact is we had a long relationship, David and I. I told you he asked me to marry him, but I didn't tell you we'd been together for ages by then. It was all terribly terribly discreet and I don't think anybody knew. We were both free at the time and doing nothing wrong, but David was of the opinion that it was an impossible situation to have a sexual relationship with a colleague, particularly as I was a very lowly trainee at the time. It was quite exciting in fact because we had to keep our distance at work and I think we did that so well that nobody had a clue. We didn't live together but I used to spend time at the house. I had always admired him of course from afar, but I didn't realise for some time that he was looking at me in that way so it was a bit of a mystery how we ever got together. He was in his late forties at the time which seemed very old to a girl in her twenties and perhaps that was why he didn't want people to know. It's funny how times have changed.'

'It still matters. He never spoke to me about you, not in that sense,' Francesca said quietly, recalling the dinner parties at Selina's, the friendly banter between the two of them that never suggested anything else. 'It was no secret that we both had relationships before, but that was to be expected at our age and I really did not want to know details.'

'No, well ... I told him it was probably best if he didn't mention it. And there was something else too.'

'I thought there might be. What?'

'I became pregnant,' she said blushing to the roots of her fair hair. 'We'd only known each other for a while and it was not planned.'

'Oh. Did you tell him?'

'No. I dealt with it as he would have wanted me to do if he had known.'

'That's not fair. Surely he suspected something?'

She shook her head. 'No. You know David, he never took a great deal of notice of *female* happenings.'

'He would have been pleased surely. It wasn't as if he was married or anything. There was no reason why you shouldn't marry.'

'There was every reason. I didn't want him to think I had trapped him. I've seen it happen to other people and it always turns sour in the end. He didn't want to get married. He wasn't ready for marriage.'

'He was in his forties for heaven's sake.'

'Yes, but he wasn't ready.'

'But he did ask you, didn't he, and you turned him down? You've only yourself to blame, Selina.'

'I didn't explain it very well. Yes he did propose some time after the abortion and I asked for time to consider it, but I only did that because I didn't want to appear too keen. I ask you, playing hard to get after all that time together. It was ludicrous but we always danced round each other like that. The truth was neither of us was ready for commitment, darling. But I was so excited when he finally got round to it and next morning I made up my mind to say yes and then he came up to me in court of all places, not actually in court itself that would have been a nonsense but outside in the gallery whilst we were waiting and …' she sighed. 'He took me to one side and said that he was sorry about last night and he got carried away and of course it was ridiculous to think of us marrying so would I just forget it. In other words, he had bloody second thoughts and retracted the question before I had the chance to say yes.'

'Why didn't you tell him that? Good heavens, Selina, you knew him well enough.'

'And have him retract the retraction? No way would I do that but I ended it at that point because it was quite clear it was going nowhere and I had put myself through an abortion for that man. I shall never forgive myself for doing that. It was probably the daughter I will never have.' On cue her eyes filled with tears and she rummaged in her designer handbag for a tissue.

'You don't know that.'

'I met Clive six weeks later and I was so miserable I allowed him to sweep me off my feet. Well, sort of. You know Clive. He's hardly the sweeping-off-the-feet type.'

'You two are great together. You're lucky, Selina.'

'As to the paintings, I'm sorry to keep harping on about them but the truth is David did promise me them. He knew I liked them.'

'Did you really like them?' Francesca said. 'Didn't I hear you say they were utter crap.'

'That's Clive. He's got a closed mind where modern art is concerned. No imagination at all. I loved them. Anyway, before you came on the scene David once said that if he popped off ...' she shuddered and bit her lip. 'I was to have them and I said that he should put that in writing.'

'He did leave a will,' Francesca reminded her.

'Which he only got round to making after you married him.' The accusation hung there.

'I didn't ask him to do that. I did say I was surprised he hadn't made one already and that must have shocked him into doing it.'

'I was so hurt that after all we went through together he left me nothing, nothing at all to remember him by. Instead, he left it all to you. Somebody who knew him all of five minutes.'

'Somebody he *married*.' Francesca was finding it difficult to hold onto her temper. 'Why didn't you ask me? I would have given them to you. They meant very little to me.'

'I know they didn't and that was another thing that hurt. At least I shared David's passion for them.'

'That's why you were so keen to know what I intended to do with them?'

'Yes, I had to intervene otherwise you might have sent them in a job lot to the local Oxfam shop.'

'I might have but I don't think I would. I'm not as naïve as you seem to think. I knew they had a value.'

'As you were giving the money you got from the paintings to charity I couldn't make a fuss and I thought that if I couldn't have them then at least some good was coming out of it. I support those two particular charities myself,' she added with a sudden steely glint in her eyes. 'So that, darling, is when I saw red. There have been no sizeable donations from you recently and it's some considerable time since the paintings were sold.'

'You had no business to check up. I thought donations were private matters.'

'They are but I wheedled it out of someone. It was pretty unethical and I only did it because I wanted to be sure that David's express wishes were being upheld,' she said, taking on her solicitor voice.

'If you had talked to me,' Francesca said, quiet and determined and furious by then. 'If you had done me the honour of trusting me ...' now she was being as formal as Selina, but stupidly she was more concerned now that she was going to lose her composure and start crying which would be such a waste. 'I would have explained. After the auction, I put the money aside if you must know, the bulk of it anyway. I have it earmarked for a project of my own which I am not going to go into, but I certainly intend to give the sizeable donations you speak of to David's charities when the shares are sorted out. It's just a bit of juggling that's all, a temporary thing and they won't lose out. I am not using the money for myself, Selina. Do you really want to know what I'm using it for?'

'No.' Selina held up her hand. 'Sorry, sorry, sorry. It's none of my business.'

'No it isn't.' For the first time it occurred that Selina was not a friend like Izzy, just a mere acquaintance because she knew nothing of her background, of what went before. 'Why did you say those things to Gareth?'

'Can't you guess? Because I was jealous ...' she said. 'I was so bloody jealous and I wanted to spoil it for you. Good Lord, Francesca, you pinched David from me.'

'Can you hear yourself? You were married to Clive at the

time. How could I pinch David from you?' Francesca could not help herself. She laughed at the stupidity of it. How could a grown up, a professional at that, behave like a little girl?

'I know I'm not making sense, but I married Clive on the rebound. And for God's sake don't tell him that either.'

'Why did you introduce us in the first place? If I remember, you were dead set on doing it.'

'I know I was. You aren't going to believe this, but I planned it. It sounds perfectly ridiculous now.'

'Try me.'

'I could read the man's mind. I was furious because after I ditched him he bounced back so quickly. Clearly, he was hardly heartbroken, as I was. After me, there had been one or two little flings, but I knew that those women did not mean much to him. I was waiting for the moment when he fell in love with someone as I fell in love with him. And then you came along. I knew he wanted you because I saw him watching you at that children's cancer charity function where I first saw you. It was back in the November. We didn't actually speak at the time, but you were there with that red-head friend of yours. You know the girl ... fat with the most God-awful hair-do.'

'Mary?'

'Yes, Mary.'

'I remember the function.' She recalled now that when she first met Selina she half thought that she had seen her some-where before. 'Was David there?'

'You bet he was and he couldn't take his eyes off you. All bloody night. I was wearing this terrific little number but he never gave me a second glance and that hurt. I know I finished our affair but I couldn't stop playing up to him whenever I saw him. Didn't you notice?'

'No.'

She laughed. 'Neither did David. I was really wasting my time, wasn't I? I did expect him to be a bit jealous of me and Clive but he wasn't in the least.'

'Didn't Clive mind you flirting?'

'He didn't know. But my efforts were wasted that evening and I ended up watching him watching you. We were on the same table. Don't you remember? You were sitting next to Mary and David was more or less opposite. Didn't you speak?'

'It was a big table,' she said stupidly. 'I don't remember him.'

'Well, you certainly made an impact on him. It was a real Cinderella moment. He wore his heart on his sleeve did David. It was some enchanted evening stuff, across the crowded room and all that jazz.'

'I never knew I was being watched,' Francesca said, smiling a little.

'You don't realize, Francesca, how attractive you are to the opposite sex.' Selina smiled ruefully.

'Why didn't he make it his business to speak to me? Why didn't he introduce himself?'

'That's not his way. I expect he needed time to himself to think about it. Was this finally it? Had he met his Miss Right at last? He collared me at work next day and immediately asked if I knew you.'

'Me?'

'Of course you. He wanted to know who you were, whether you were married or engaged and how he could get in touch with you. And so I told him I knew that you were a single lady and could arrange an introduction. I didn't actually know you at the time, but I knew Mary vaguely and knew I could get to know you through her.'

'Why?'

'Because I knew he had fallen for you – he was such an old

romantic as you know – so I wanted to hurt him, to let him know how it felt to be cold shouldered by somebody you love, the way he had to me. I wanted to give him a taste of his own medicine. My God, he never knew how much I was hurt. I might have had his child, Francesca. So, I wanted to get back at him. I know it's unbelievably childish, but I'm like that. It's really beneath me. I imagined that you would give him the brush-off pretty damned quick, an old man like that. What I didn't bargain for was that you would fall in love with him or think you did. That really made it all go belly up and when he told me he was going to marry you I had no alternative, but to accept it as gracefully as I could.' She rooted through her bag, got out another tissue and blew her nose hard. 'And then I go and do it again, but this time I was trying to spoil it for you and Gareth just because I was pissed off about the sodding paintings. Oh God, shoot me now. I will of course apologize to him if you'll let me.'

'No need. He didn't believe you anyway.'

'Good.' She tugged at her hair. 'Look at me. I haven't washed my hair for two days. I dared not stop for a cup of tea on the way because I look such a fright.'

It was *so* Selina.

'You look awful,' Francesca confirmed with some satisfaction.

'I look my age,' she said. 'And I'm going to do something about it. I'm having some work done to my face. I'm told it hurts like hell so I'm bracing myself. It will give my skin a glow. It's costing, darling, so I hope it will be worth it. Don't tell Clive.'

'Won't he notice?'

'By the time he gets back the bruising will be easing and I can always say I walked into a door or fell over one of the blasted cats. He won't notice anyway. Men never do. It's my women friends who will notice which beggars the question who am I doing this for?'

'Yourself?'

So maybe the dash home was not entirely for her benefit, not if she had a pre-booked clinic appointment.

'Are we still friends?'

'Oh Selina … Can I be honest?'

'Of course.'

'You are right about one thing. I rushed into it and I was having doubts. I don't believe I would have ever settled up in Yorkshire and spending the rest of my life just being Mrs David Porter would have driven me mad sooner rather than later. I married him because he wouldn't take no for an answer, but that doesn't stop me missing him.'

'I know. And I am so sorry. Will you ever forgive me? Can I stay tonight? Please don't send me off looking for somewhere to stay looking like I do.'

'Yes, you can stay. And go and wash your hair for goodness sake. What *are* you wearing?' she added, taking stock of the outfit for the first time

'Hideous, isn't it? I couldn't be arsed when I got home to put things together properly. I just threw an overnight into the car and drove like the wind. I was desperate to get here. Am I forgiven? Or do I have to prostrate myself at your feet because I will if you want me to?'

'Don't be daft.'

'What about you and Gareth then?' A twinkle returned to her eyes. 'You never told me he was such a hunk.'

'Hardly.' She knew she was blushing. 'That isn't important anyway. He's very nice. He could have kept all that to himself but he told me because he thought I ought to know.

Incidentally …' a thought struck her. 'How did you know that he had told me?'

'He doesn't look the sort who can keep a secret and you hadn't phoned for a while, the silence was deafening, so I figured that he must have told you. Clive had one of his business cards so I called him just to confirm it. He told me not to come here under any circumstances.' She laughed. 'He was very forceful. I love that in a man. I could fall for him myself if I wasn't so blissfully happily married,' she said, sarcasm at full stretch.

They had both loved David and who knows maybe Selina had loved him most of all.

She would forgive Selina because David would want her to.

And also, she had to show herself that she was not like her mother who had never, not even at the very last, forgiven *her*.

As he lay dying, even as words finally deserted him, her father had motioned her to come close and somehow drummed up the energy to ask her to forgive him.

And she had.

Now all that remained was for James to forgive *her*.

Chapter Twenty

ALAN WAS NOTHING like the man she had imagined him to be.

She had expected a quiet man, a perfect foil for his wife not a short heavily built man every bit as chatty and effervescent as Izzy and it made for a noisy and happily chaotic relationship.

'So you couldn't resist moving back to Devon?' he asked when he met her in the hall of Gareth's cottage, having greeted her with a bear hug. 'Good for you. There's no place like home, eh? Sorry to hear about your husband. Izzy told me. Bad luck.'

'Sorry about the mess.' Izzy pulled a face, looking harassed as she tidied things away. 'Don't tell Gareth what a pickle it's in. I promise I'll give it a good clean before we leave. This is what it's like when you have kids, Francesca.' She spun round as little Mabel hugged her leg, whipping the child up into her arms and laughing at her as she gave her a big kiss. 'Say hello to Auntie Francesca, Sweetheart.'

'That's too complicated for her,' Alan said as Mabel stuck her thumb in her mouth before looking at her with great suspicion. 'Do you get called Fran?

'Never.' Izzy answered for her. 'Everybody calls her Francesca. Come on, let's get going or we'll never get there.'

'Can I help?' Francesca stood helplessly by as Izzy started to hand things out to all and sundry, including Mabel who was in charge of her bucket and spade.

'Absolutely. Take this,' Izzy said, handing her a huge picnic bag.

'Wagons roll. Let's go, ladies.' Alan announced with a big grin and they set off, Alan leading the way and she and Izzy bringing up the rear.

Gareth had recommended visiting a nearby beach which was particularly recommended for children with a safe shallow stretch of water and some rock pools; the only problem being it was tricky to get to as it was down a lot of steps. Even though Izzy had apparently invited him, Gareth did not join them, deciding wisely that they had a lot of catching up to do and he would just get in the way.

'What a considerate man. I should hold onto him if I were you,' Izzy said with a smile.

'He's not mine to hold onto,' Francesca whispered, needing to make things clear.

'Isn't he?' The smile widened. 'Haven't you noticed the way he looks at you? Alan used to look at me like that. He still does sometimes although we don't have much time these days for romantic get-togethers. I long for the days when there are just the two of us again,' Izzy said as they strolled along, Vicky in front of them with Sarah and Jane and Alan forging ahead carrying Mabel aloft. 'That was before we were married of course. I was already pregnant when I got married so we didn't have long to wait before there were three of us. Then four, five and now six.'

'You're so lucky, Izzy, to have a man like Alan.'

'I know. Now that we've met up again, you and me, now that you're going to be living fairly close to us, we really must keep in touch. No more excuses,' Izzy said. 'By the way, Vicky thinks you're very cool.'

'Does she? I can't think why.'

'You had a fabulous job in London in advertising, that's why. She thinks that sounds really glamorous. I'm her mum and I haven't done anything remotely interesting so obviously I'm very un-cool.'

'It wasn't glamorous at all, just hard work although I have to say I did get a buzz out of it.'

'Do you miss that? The buzz?'

'I suppose so.'

Trust Izzy to come up with that, to make her realize what was missing these days in her life. It was the buzz, the excitement, the nervous anticipation, the thrill when it went right, the agony when it didn't.

That was what she needed in her life. Izzy was happy with her lot, but she needed something completely different.

They stopped chatting as they reached the top of the steps where some care had to be taken particularly with Mabel and Jane. At the bottom of the steps the sand was soft and ankle deep and they struggled through it to set up camp on firmer ground. Then followed all the usual fuss associated with a large family. Windbreak, chairs, assorted bags and no sooner had they settled having marked out their territory then Izzy was up again, changing Mabel into her swimsuit so that she could play in the nearby rock pool and then, minutes later, she was delving into the picnic bag for sandwiches.

'Can't you sit still for a minute? We've only just got here,' Francesca said, chastising her gently.

'I know but I've been up since six o'clock. I'm starving,' Izzy said, biting into a thickly filled sandwich. 'Want one? Help yourself. There's enough to feed an army.'

Francesca shook her head and began the serious job of applying sun-cream. Izzy started on a hefty paperback and Francesca lay down and relaxed for a while, enjoying the gentle warmth of the sun, until she was woken from her reverie by some serious rustling beside her.

'I don't know if I dare be seen in this bikini,' Izzy whispered. 'I've gone up a dress size since I bought it. I tried it on the other day and it is nothing short of horrific. Alan says I look great, but he wouldn't dare say anything else.'

'You look just fine,' Francesca reassured her, catching a glimpse of a lot of flesh as, with the finesse of a magician, Izzy cast aside her cover-up.

'Not as fine as you. But then, you haven't had any kids, Francesca, and boy does it show.'

Just for a minute, there was in the voice a touch of the old Izzy who had not been averse to the odd sly remark. Francesca glanced at her sharply before deciding that nothing malicious had been intended.

They settled down to some serious sun worshipping.

Alan and the girls had gone off to the little beach shop at the very end of the beach, a Sahara-like trek with little Mabel gallantly sifting her way through the deep sand. Feeling the waves of silent sympathy coming her way, Francesca at last took the opportunity to talk about David and Izzy let her do it, keeping quiet and allowing her to get it off her chest.

'He sounds quite a man,' Izzy said after a while. 'He wouldn't have been easy I can tell that, but it would have worked out if the two of you loved each other.'

'Would it?'

'Of course it would. Don't you think that I haven't had doubts over the years? Everybody does sometime or other. I often wish I'd married somebody with money for one thing or somebody with a bit of a romantic streak in them. Alan always forgets my birthday and our anniversary and at first I was fighting mad about it, but now I know he doesn't mean anything and Vicky's been reminding him for the last few years. It's a woman's thing, isn't it, remembering dates? It's our bodies I suppose. We have to work to a monthly schedule.'

'David was good with dates,' Francesca said. 'Although I think his assistant jogged his memory. He sent me a beautiful bouquet of flowers every Friday.'

'Why Friday?'

'Why not?'

'That would have irritated me after a while. I like a bit of spontaneity. Flowers every Friday means he's just put an order into the florists. He's not really thinking about it. Sorry.'

'You're right,' Francesca thought about Gareth and the bunch of flowers bought on impulse from the market.

'Sorry, I didn't mean to sound as if I was criticizing him. Do you miss him?' she asked at last. 'Sorry again, that's a daft question. Of course you do.'

'But I have to move on. Other people do.'

'Of course you must and don't feel guilty about doing that,' Izzy told her. 'From what you say he loved you and he would want you to be happy again. What about Gareth?'

'What about him?'

'Just that he seems a nice man. That's all.'

'He is. He's asked me out for dinner.'

'I hope you said yes?'

She nodded. 'But now I'm wondering if I did the right thing. I've only been a widow a few months.'

'So what? You mustn't let the opportunity pass you by. Don't let this guilt get to you as well.'

'As well as what?'

'You know what I'm talking about, the guilt you feel, the guilt we all feel about what happened to James. And you must not think for a minute that your mother did not know the truth. She never believed me.'

'Didn't she? We never talked about it. I once tried, but she didn't want to know the details. There was no point, she said. It was done and it couldn't be undone.'

'There you are then. Mothers know everything. In the end it didn't matter, did it? It didn't matter whose idea it was to go down to the river in the first place. It didn't matter which of us wasn't watching him. And it didn't matter either who got him out of the water, which one of us got him to breathe again because we were in it together, the two of us.'

'I try to see it from her point of view. Now that you're a mother yourself, Izzy, how would you deal with it? What would you do if for example if Vicky let Mabel drown?'

'I don't know but I hope I wouldn't blame her for it if it was an accident.' She shuddered. 'I can't bear to think of it. Didn't I persuade you to go down to the river that day? I fancied bathing topless if I remember which you went all huffy about. So, if you're looking for somebody to blame it might as well be me. You can pass the guilt over if it helps.'

'No. I have to carry the can.'

'Things happen and you can't turn the clock back. We saved him anyway, between us.'

'You saved him. But as you said what was the point? So that he could spend the rest of his life damaged both mentally and physically?'

'We didn't know that. We had to try. How would we feel if we'd just walked away and left him?'

'We couldn't do that.'

'No. So we did what we thought was right at the time. Shake it off, Francesca.' She sat up in a flurry, shoulders already looking a bit red. 'What the hell are we doing dissecting all this again? Let's put it behind us. I'm not having you visiting me, Francesca Blackwell, if we're always going to be talking about it. Let's forget it. I'm going to find you a nice new man if it's the last thing I do. Maybe not Gareth but somebody like him. And, if you do get married again, I'm expecting an invitation to the wedding this time.'

'You didn't invite me to *your* wedding,' Francesca reminded her and they shared a smile keen to lighten the mood.

'It was a low-key affair. I was huge with Victoria.' She reached for the sun-cream, peering into the distance, her face lighting up. 'Oh there they are. Where the hell have they been? Do you think they need a hand? Alan looks like he's bought the entire shop.'

'I'll go.' Francesca rose, dusted off the sand, slipping her cover-up on over her one-piece swimsuit. 'You wait here.'

She set off to meet Alan. She had enjoyed the day, but she would have to get herself home soon although she would be back on Friday afternoon for her dinner date with Gareth.

The floral sheaf knee-length dress was one that Selina had nudged her into buying; it was a touch retro and city chic, even if it did resemble a pair of Pamela's curtains, but its very exuberance did have the effect of drawing attention away from her flushed face. With it, she wore high-heeled silver sandals and as she fastened the clasp on her necklace, one of David's expensive gifts, Francesca felt light hearted and even a little light headed. She put it down to too much sun over the last few days.

Tonight would be her first proper date since David and it felt odd in an excited teenage first-date way. Gareth was taking her to a swanky hotel nearby, a large Victorian hotel perched on the cliff edge with enviable views of a long stretch of sand and the sort of rolling sea that made it popular with surfers.

He had booked a table on the veranda so that they might watch the sun setting. He had also arranged that she stay overnight with Izzy at the cottage to save her the bother of driving home. It also meant that with a taxi ferrying them back and forth, they could enjoy a drink or two.

'I'm not sure how you will take this, but you can stay with me at the caravan if you want,' he told her on the way there. 'You are very welcome. You can have the double in the bedroom and I'll bunk down on the pull-out in the lounge. Either that or you can stay at the cottage and share a room with Mabel. Your choice.'

Did she detect an amused tone? Why the hell didn't he come right out with it and ask her to sleep with him?

She was non-committal, more than a little mortified that he should need to make the sleeping arrangements this evening quite so crystal clear. They were grown-ups, they were attracted to each other and there was no point in denying that and neither of them had had sex for a while. At least she could only speak for herself on that one, but Gareth had not mentioned anybody else. So, opting for the too cosy caravan setting seemed a completely barmy idea because if the dining experience was anything like he was promising – delicious food, wine and a beautiful sunset – there was only one possible outcome.

Francesca felt sure of one thing. Izzy would be extremely disappointed if she turned up on the cottage doorstep at midnight.

The view from the veranda was spectacular made even more so by the balminess of the evening air. The sea cooling down from the heat of the day was a rippling silvery gleam, the horizon a pinkish purple, the sun a golden bowl low in the sky. There were candles in silver holders on the table, little pots of fresh flowers, and the air was still. It was sheltered out here with leafy vine-filled walls mingling with flowering climbers twisted round the hefty wooden pillars around and above them.

It was one of those moments of rare perfection.

'Well … what do you think?'

'I think it's breathtaking.'

'And so are you,' he whispered on cue, but somehow the predictability of the remark did not matter and tonight Francesca determined she was not going to start comparisons between this man and David.

'I'm looking for a job,' she said as they waited for their starters. 'Either that or I'm going to start up in business.'

'Sounds good. Doing what?'

'I don't know. But I have been doing a bit of research looking for a gap in the market and I think I might have found one. We don't have a shop in town that specialises in fine art. I could do that. I don't know a thing about it, but I could find somebody who does. I have the money to fund it and I believe there would be a market for it.'

'Lucky you.'

Against her better judgement, she bristled at that, at what she considered to be a flippant remark.

'Don't start behaving like Selina acting as if I'm just playing at it because I don't know how to spend my money,' she told him sharply. 'I know I would have trouble doing this without David's money, but it's hardly my fault if he wanted me to have it, is it? And he would be pleased if he knew that I was doing something with it, something to help out talented young artists just like he used to do.'

'Don't be so defensive.' He smiled and took her hand. 'Look, I told you I didn't believe that woman. Anyway, I thought you two were friends again?'

'We are,' she said, knowing though that, despite the goodbye hug she and Selina had shared, things would never be exactly as they were. 'Don't let's talk about her, not tonight.'

'I couldn't agree more. So … you're thinking of opening a gallery? Have you spotted any premises?'

She nodded. 'A choice of two. One's in a prime position but the other is probably better suited to what I have in mind.'

'We'll have to take a run to St Ives and we can look at the galleries together to give you some ideas how you might present yours. We might get the chance to talk to some local artists. I'm sure they would be delighted to exhibit.'

'Thanks. That would be good.'

'And it goes without saying that if you want any help in the business line, drawing up contracts and so on then you need look no further.'

She nodded. She had something to prove and wanted to do it herself, but it was good to know that an expert was on hand if she needed him.

'You know, Gareth, I wish I'd kept the paintings now that it's too late. I never understood David's taste and it could be I was a bit dismissive. I'd like to try and understand it more. After all, my mother was an artist with a considerable talent, but she doesn't seem to have passed it on to me.'

'Yes she has. You are creative, aren't you?'

'In a different sense.'

'Anyway it doesn't always follow. *My* mother's a musician, but I'm tone deaf.'

'It's something I can get my teeth into. I could start by selling some of the work of the artists David supported …' she paused, aware that she might be mentioning him far too much. 'Anyway, it's early days, but it's an idea for me to think about.'

'And a good one. It's good to set yourself a target and do something outside your comfort zone.'

The wine waiter arrived, doing his stuff in a very flamboyant way, and, catching her eye Gareth winked. Somehow, the little gesture set the tone of the evening and she determined to relax and let it take its course. She was fed up with analysing every aspect of her life and it was time she acted once again on impulse, doing what felt right. Time also that she did not put David centre stage the whole time for the worst thing she could think of, if positions were reversed was if Gareth kept going on and on about a woman he had once loved. After that initial mention of the woman called Helen he had not spoken of her again.

'Gareth ...' she reached out to touch his hand. 'Thank you. This is really very nice.'

She wished she could think of something more profound, but it would have to do and, as their eyes met, she was sure he had got the message.

They had requested a few minutes respite before the dessert menu was brought to them. The meal so far had been wonderful and, although it was cooling down now, it was still most pleasant. As the sun slipped out of sight, the sky was now a fantastic mix of colours. Francesca slipped a feathery light wrap round her shoulders to ward off the chill and they decided that, after dessert, they would take the waiter's advice and move inside to the lounge to take coffee. Francesca's mind was made up; she had decided to stay with Gareth tonight and, judging from his cat-that-got-the-cream look, he knew it.

After dessert, as they waited in the lounge for the coffee, it started to go wrong.

It began with a casual mention from Gareth about his brother Simon who lived in the States.

'I didn't know you had a brother,' she said.

'It never came up. You have a brother too, don't you?'

'How do you know that?' she asked more sharply than she intended.

'You mentioned him when we had dinner with Pamela and Richard.'

Ah yes.

'It's not something I want to talk about,' she said, sensing a question coming on.

'I gathered that. Family rift?' he asked sympathetically. 'Don't worry. It happens in all families. In fact it would probably happen in mine if the two of us didn't live so far apart that we hardly ever see each other.'

'It's not a family rift. Not with James. The rift was between me and my mother. She's dead now so there's no way it can ever be resolved. She never forgave me. Look ..' she glanced round. 'Would you mind, Gareth, if we skip the coffee? I need to talk and we can't do it here.'

'No problem.' He signalled to the waiter.

It was chilly standing in the porch waiting for the taxi and they said little on the short journey back.

'Thanks for a lovely evening,' she said, once the taxi had dropped them off. She could see that a light was on in one of the cottage's windows. 'I hope Izzy hasn't stayed up waiting for me.'

'I shouldn't think so. Come on, I'll make us coffee,' he said, putting his arm on her waist. 'You look cold. Stay with me tonight.'

'I'm not in the mood,' she said abruptly, shaking him off. 'I'm sorry, Gareth. I will stay, but you must understand that ...' she struggled to say it, contenting herself with simply patting his arm and smiling up at him.

'Not to worry.' He smiled wryly as they made their way over to the caravan. 'We have all the time in the world.'

Chapter Twenty One

GARETH MADE COFFEE. It was not the best idea at this hour, but Francesca needed it, a good strong cup of black coffee.

'In your own time,' he said. 'And don't spare me the details. I can take it.'

She started off by telling him about James's accident, exactly what had happened and how useless she had been, how she felt totally responsible for the injury she had caused him and how she had ruined her little brother's life, not to mention her mother's.

'Izzy did her best. She tried to help by telling Mother that it was I who rescued him, implying of course that I had jumped in straightaway as any sane sister would have done. And then the local paper got hold of it and made me out to be a heroine forgetting to mention that James was going to be permanently handicapped. People were congratulating me for heaven's sake. And I let them.'

'Once you start these balls rolling you can't stop them. Where is he now?'

'He's in a special nursing home in Kent.' She blinked back sudden, stinging tears. 'After Mother died, it was the best I could do. I couldn't look after him properly, not when I was working and everything, but it quickly swallowed up what bit of money Mother had left him. I had hoped that after I married

David he would be happy for me to move James nearer to us up in Yorkshire. Once I got round to telling him that is.'

'And now?'

'He's coming home,' she said firmly. 'I've earmarked the big room for him and I shall get a full-time carer in and she can have the smaller room and, please don't look like that, Gareth, I have to have a carer because it's just too much for me to look after him myself. He's over six feet tall and heavy.'

'Of course it's too much. I wasn't judging you for a minute. We would all like to do the caring ourselves, but it is better that he's looked after professionally.'

'And what do you know about it? Have you done a course in counselling?'

'No.' He flushed, taken aback no doubt at the aggressive tone.

'Sorry. I'm a bit touchy about it. He will have the best of care now that I can afford it. I've earmarked the money I got from selling off David's paintings to pay for that. James will want for nothing for as long as he lives and I've even made arrangements for his continuing care if anything happens to me.'

'Why the hell didn't you tell Selina this?'

'Because I haven't been able to talk to anybody about it. Nobody except Izzy. I didn't even talk to David about it. He thought I was an only child. He thought both my parents were dead as his were.'

'And weren't they?'

'Well yes, now they are. My dad ...' she hesitated but she couldn't stop now and before she knew it she had told him everything.

'You poor love,' he smiled and gathered her into his arms as she finished. 'My God, you've gone through it recently.'

'I feel all right about my dad,' she said, mumbling into his shoulder. 'I'm glad I saw him again and I'm glad that he forgave my mother. I never thought he cared about either of us and it turned out that he did. And now, if I can do something for James it will help me, help both of us. I want him to come home.'

'Have you visited him?'

She nodded. 'It's painful. I don't think he knew who I was. He smiled and was very nice and friendly but I think he thought I was just another lady who sits and chats to him. There was no recognition at all.'

'I'm sure he knows deep down.'

'I helped him do a jigsaw puzzle. He just stuffed the pieces into the wrong places like a child. I hope to goodness he knows it is home when he gets here. I'm worried sick that he'll hate it and want to go back to the other place where he's happy and I'm scared that he'll think I'm a stranger.' she stood up, exhausted suddenly, and needing her bed. 'Where am I sleeping?'

'With me, my darling,' he said softly. He shifted slightly so that he could look at her, smiling and wiping away a stray tear. 'I'm not leaving you alone tonight.'

Tearfully but happily, she raised her face to be kissed.

Izzy caught up with her next day. She had started packing prior to their leaving and she said she was both sad to be leaving, but pleased to be going home.

'There'll be mountains of washing,' she said. 'But it'll be great to be back in our own bed with our own pillows and duvet. There's nothing quite like your own bed.'

Francesca nodded. It was a very middle-aged comment and she was amazed that Izzy, the wonderful energetic Izzy, had uttered it. She knew that Izzy was hoping she would tell her what had happened between her and Gareth last night but she felt like a shy teenager again and did not feel up to discussing it.

It had been a powerfully emotional experience, her senses were on a high as a result of all that had happened to her which therefore took it to an entirely new level. Of course being in a caravan meant little privacy and she could hear and smile at the sounds Gareth was making in the little galley which were followed eventually by a breakfast tray in bed.

'I don't do this for anybody,' he said as he proudly set it down. 'Just for the ladies I sleep with.'

She laughed and pretended to throw the pillow at him, finding that she was surprisingly hungry and deftly demolishing the scrambled eggs he had prepared.

'Don't go yet,' he implored after she had showered and dressed.

'I'll be back,' she assured him. 'I need time to think. Please don't make me stay.'

Perversely half of her wanted him to do just that for she knew that it would only take a little persuading, but he did not. It was when she was putting her bag in her car that Izzy collared her.

'I hope you weren't sneaking off,' she said.

'No, I was going to pop in to see you before I go,' Francesca told her, not entirely sure she had been. 'It's early, Izzy, I didn't want to disturb you.'

'Early? You are joking. If I wake up at seven, I've had a lie in. We aren't going until midday so I'm leaving Victoria to cook them breakfast and having a final walk along the cliffs on my own. Want to come with me?'

Francesca looked up at the grey sky. The weather had changed overnight and it was chilly with a big bank of clouds overhead and darker more ominous ones in the distance.

'It's going to rain,' she told Izzy.

'So what?' Izzy was wearing cropped pants, stretched tight across her bottom, with a lightweight anorak over them and, make-up free she looked dumpy and mumsy and yet, underneath it all, she looked tanned, relaxed and happy and having seen her with her children, Francesca knew that her maternal instincts, so ingrained and recognizable at a young age, had been satisfied. Hers had never existed and that was the way it was and the way it would be. There was no time for regrets.

'Come on, it will do us good. We won't go far and if it does rain I've got a brolly.'

'You've been lucky with the weather. Have you enjoyed your holiday?' Francesca asked as they set off down the track.

'It's been great. It's back to work next week. Alan has got a big painting job and I've got a lot of paperwork to sort out.'

They fell into a comfortable silence, tramping uphill, puffing a bit.

'I'm glad you've moved back here,' Izzy said at last. 'I never thought you would. I understand that completely, but to move back to your old house just seems crazy to me. All those awful memories.'

'There were some good ones too. I love it down here, Izzy, and you must understand that. I'm not sure I'm doing the right thing but I'm bringing James back to live at the house. I shall have help with him,' she added quickly.

'I should hope so. There's nothing to be gained by being a martyr to the cause.'

'That's what Gareth says.'

'You could do worse than him.' She glanced sharply at her.

'I've only known him a little while.'

'And?' Izzy grinned. 'It's happened, hasn't it? Don't you dare deny it, I can tell just by looking at you. Was it good?'

'Don't be so nosy.'

They laughed and, as of old, the disgracefully indiscreet Izzy tucked her arm in Francesca's telling her that it was still pretty fantastic with Alan, although they hardly ever got time these days as they normally had at least two of the girls coming into their bed at some time during the night.

They had walked further than they intended and were very nearly at the cliff edge, out of sight of the cottage when the first spots of rain fell and, in the distance, thunder rumbled.

'Oh God, we're not going to have lightning, are we?' Francesca asked.

'Probably, but there's no need to panic. Don't tell me you're still scared of thunder?' she glanced at Francesca, one look all she needed to confirm it. 'OK. I don't think we should try to go back because we'll get caught out in the open. We'll take shelter.'

'Where? Don't be daft. There's nowhere *to* shelter, Izzy.'

Within minutes, horrifyingly quickly, the rain started pelting down in earnest and with the advancing storm the sky turned a peculiar yellow colour. It was more like early evening than early morning as Francesca quickly followed Izzy down the path to the beach and the shelter of a little cave. Underneath their feet the sand here was gritty with crunchy shells by the entrance and inside it smelled of seaweed and damp sand. Lying across a flat stone was a child's lost sock, a white one with pink edging. They could see the sea, a murky dishwater of a sea, the waves rolling in, but not in any sinister way. It looked no worse than usual out there.

'This is creepy.' Francesca shuddered, looking round. 'How did you know about this?'

'I make it my business to know. Gareth told me about it and

we're perfectly safe and no the sea won't come in this far so we're not going to get cut off. Oh, there's the lightning.'

There indeed was the lightning and Francesca, even though she tried, could not help a little yelp of fear.

'Oh for goodness sake, you're as bad as my kids. Do you want a cuddle?' Izzy asked with a grin. 'Or are you a big girl now?'

Francesca managed a smile. 'I'm all right,' she said, although she was nervously counting seconds before the next rumble of thunder.

'We have about as much chance of being hit by lightning as *you* have of having twins. Have a Polo.' Izzy handed her a mint. 'It's circling us but we'll wait a bit to make sure. It's just an overhead storm and it will soon pass and I wouldn't be at all surprised if we see a rainbow when the sun comes out,' she added in an authoritative voice as if she was a meteorologist.

'Are you sure it's passing over?' Francesca asked, needing assurance.

'Absolutely. It's heading inland. In the meantime, we can have a nice chat,' she said, taking off her anorak and laying it on the rock, moving the sock as she did so. She was wearing open toed sandals and her feet were gritty and dirty. Her hair was unruly and she was not wearing make-up but hell … her face was a lot smoother than Selina's and it was something to do with serenity. Izzy, for all the chaos in her life, was doing what she wanted to do. Izzy was also with the man she loved. 'Sit down and tell me what happened last night. You were back early and you both looked a little tense.'

'Were you spying on us?'

'No but I just happened to glance out of the window when I heard voices,' she said airily. 'You weren't holding hands and you were striding along and I thought … oops, this doesn't look good. Did you have a row?'

'Not exactly. It was lovely at first,' Francesca said, trapped but feeling better as the worst of the thunder and lightning seemed to be easing. 'We dined out on the veranda and it was a gorgeous sunset.'

'Yes I remember. We sat out a while too, just me and Alan, although he didn't notice the sunset. He's not into sunsets. Go on, tell me what happened.'

'It started off so well, but the conversation turned to family and brothers and it just killed the mood.'

'Did you tell him about James?'

She nodded.

'Good. I'm glad. It must mean something, Francesca, if you told him. You never plucked up the courage to tell your husband, did you?'

She shook her head. 'I was going to but I never did. I don't know what he would have made of it. I don't like to say this, but he wasn't very patient with ill-health or disabled people. He was never rude but not particularly patient. I think I knew that it would never work, James coming to live with us, and maybe that's why I didn't tell him because I couldn't have borne it if he had said no. It's different with Gareth. Gareth understands.'

Izzy peeped out from their cave. 'Look, it was just a flash in the pan. It's clearing up already. Come on, we'll get ourselves back.'

'Go with your instincts,' Izzy told her on the return trip, tramping across the damp field. 'It's no earthly use asking me. It's what you feel that matters. If he's the one for you then go for it. Don't start analyzing it too much because that never works. Heart over head that's what you have to do.'

'Like buying a house? I knew I wanted to buy the house as

soon as Gareth told me it was for sale. It was mad, impulsive, stupid, all of that but I just went ahead and bought it.'

Izzy glanced at her. 'Do you want to know a secret?'

'A good one?'

'Yes. So far as I'm concerned anyway. Alan will take a little winning round, but …' she hesitated. 'I'm pregnant.'

'Again?'

'Yes and don't say it like that. It's only just happened, but I always know well in advance. Perhaps it will be a boy this time, but if it isn't, it doesn't matter. Of course it will put my plans back a little because I don't want to start the course whilst I'm pregnant but who cares?'

'I'm happy for you if that's what you want.' Francesca smiled at her. 'Perhaps I might be able to help out a bit now that we don't live so far apart. Babysitting and stuff.'

'Thanks. Vicky will be horrified, of course. She's at that age when she thinks it is positively disgusting that her parents might still be having sex. And don't say anything to Alan, not yet.'

'Of course I won't.'

And she would not.

The two of them were good at keeping secrets.

They were nearly back at the cottage and they could see Alan beginning to load up the car.

'I'll leave you to it,' Francesca told her as they gave each other a goodbye hug.

'Keep in touch.'

'You bet.'

She left them to walk over to Gareth's caravan where he was waiting for her.

'Where have you been?' he said, rushing down the little steps. 'I was getting worried about you out in that weather.'

And that was part of it, she thought, as she followed him inside.

You only worried about somebody when you loved them.

James was due home any minute and Francesca was in a panic.

It was early September and there was a hint of autumn chill in the air so Francesca had lit a fire in the sitting room and the radiators were on everywhere else so it was nice and warm. She remembered how hot it always was in his previous place so she did not want him to be cold.

'They're here.' She heard her voice rise. 'Show them where to park, Gareth.'

And off he went, smiling at her nervousness, having tried all morning to calm her down.

What if James doesn't like it?

What if he doesn't remember it at all?

Worse, what if he still doesn't remember her?

The worries had kept her awake all night and, at the last she had dug Gareth in the ribs and woken him up and they had gone down to the kitchen and sat a while drinking hot chocolate.

Outside, in the back yard, the car drew to a halt and, standing on the step, Francesca watched as the passenger door opened and James slowly emerged, yawning, scratching his red hair – their mother's hair – and stretching his long limbs followed by the nurse and the driver. Francesca could have driven over herself and collected them but she wanted to be here to welcome them.

'All right, darling?' Gareth was at her side. He took her hand, squeezed it, and whispered that he loved her.

'I know,' she said, giving him a smile but she was distracted for now she had to concentrate all her efforts on getting this right. She stepped forward and for a minute, she was unable to move, just like before, rooted to the spot. He was so big, lumbering, just a little stooped, and he was dressed like an old man with a shirt and tie, pressed trousers and a neat old fashioned cardigan that no man of James's age would be seen dead in.

'We'll take him shopping.' Gareth said quietly at her side. 'We'll kit him out in something more appropriate. Get him some jeans for one.'

She nodded, reflecting that already they could read each other's minds.

'Look, James, there she is.' The nurse said as he stood looking round. 'There's Francesca. Do you remember me telling you about her?'

The nurse smiled at them, putting a hand on James's arms and turning him a little so that they were facing each other.

'I can't do this,' Francesca said, seeing him, a man with a little boy's mind, knowing that she was responsible for it.

'Yes you can.' With a little encouraging push from Gareth, she went forward on jelly legs.

'Welcome home, James. Do you remember Lilac House?' she asked, feeling foolish to be asking such a question of him for she didn't know quite how his mind worked these days. To her surprise, James nodded, staring at the house before holding out his hand for her to shake but, even as she took hold of it, she saw a sudden sharp recognition in his eyes and he pulled her to him in a bear hug holding her close. Perhaps it was seeing her here at the house that changed everything. Seeing her here, even though she was much changed, helped him to pinpoint just who she was.

'Frankie,' he said in a delighted voice before turning to the nurse. 'She's my big sister.'

It took all her strength not to dissolve at that moment and even the emotionally hardened nurse was finding it hard to hold onto her composure.

'It's been a long time,' Francesca whispered to him. 'How are you, James?'

'I don't know. How am I?' he looked to the nurse.

'You're fine,' she said.

'Come on, sweetheart,' Francesca said, holding him at arm's length and taking in his appearance, realizing that, for the foreseeable future, James was going to be the child she would never have. She would look after *him* for however long it took for by God she owed him that much. Turning, she saw Gareth standing waiting for them as she guided James through the door into the house.